Thicker than
Water

Thicker than
Water

·

RETT MACPHERSON

ST. MARTIN'S MINOTAUR
NEW YORK

MacPherson

www.minotaurbooks.com

Library of Congress Cataloging-in-Publication Data

MacPherson, Rett.
    Thicker than water : a Tori O'Shea mystery / Rett MacPherson.—1st St.
Martin's Minotaur ed.
        p.   cm.
    ISBN 0-312-33408-7
    EAN 978-0312-33408-6
    1. O'Shea, Torie (Fictitious character)—Fiction.   2. Inheritance and
succession—Fiction.   3. History—Societies, etc.—Fiction.   4. Women
genealogists—Fiction.   5. Home ownership—Fiction.   6. Missouri—Fiction.
I. Title.

PS3563.A3257T48   2005
813'.54—dc22

                                                            2004051414

First Edition: March 2005

10   9   8   7   6   5   4   3   2   1

To Alternate Historian

Mark Sumner

Acknowledgments

The author would like to thank the following people: Everybody at St. Martin's Press, especially my editor, Kelley Ragland, and her assistant, Carly Einstein. My agent, Merrilee Heifetz, and all the people at Writers House. You guys have been wonderful.

My writer's group, the Alternate Historians: Tom Drennan, Laurell K. Hamilton, Martha Kneib, Debbie Millitello, Sharon Shinn, and Mark Sumner for all of their endless support and help, both professional and personal.

To Evelyn Tucker, D.R.E., Sister Florence Wesselmann, SSND, and Father Edward Ramatowski of Assumption Parish, for leading the way and turning on the light. Also, thanks to all of the umpteen doctors who fixed me. (Well, okay, I'm a work in progress!) And Mr. and Mrs. Jonathan Green for immeasurable support and help this year.

And a special thank you to my husband, Joe, and to my kids for all of their love and inspiration.

Thicker than
Water

One

I think you have forgotten your promise.

I stared at the words on the postcard, all curved and fancy, in ink that at one time must have been black but now had turned a very nice Vandyke brown. The words were written about eighty years ago, according to the nearly illegibly smeared postmark. On the front of the postcard was a photograph.

A great many postcards from the first quarter of the twentieth century were photographs. I have a few in my possession, sent by my great-grandmother Bridie to a cousin of hers in California. On the front of them usually were photographs of my great-grandmother, and on the back, just a few words—sometimes just a simple *Compliments of Bridie, Panther Run, West Virginia.*

One such postcard had a photograph of the Panther Run boardinghouse with all the workers and occupants standing out front. Another was a photograph of Bridie with two neighbors and a cousin, looking simply *en vogue* in their big hats, lace-up boots, and hemlines that had crept up to their ankles.

This postcard was different. For one thing, it didn't belong to me. Well, at least not until a few weeks ago. I am Torie O'Shea, certified genealogist, which sounds much more important than it really is. Basically, it means I know how to dig around dusty old papers and records and find what people are looking for—and, more often than not, a boatload of things they're not. I'm also a tour guide for the historical society in a little German river town on the Mississippi in east-central Missouri, giving tours in its headquarters, the Gaheimer House.

At least that is who I used to be. Now I am the sole owner of the Gaheimer House and all its contents. I am nearly a millionaire if you count all of the money, property, and houses that my former boss Sylvia Pershing left me. Yes, me. Why, you ask? Hell if I know. I've been trying to figure that out myself.

Sylvia died suddenly a few weeks ago while I was on vacation with my husband, Rudy, and my stepfather, Colin. I say "suddenly," but Sylvia was 102 years old and some change. I didn't know exactly how old she was until after she was dead. I can't express how much it bothered me that her hundredth birthday had come and gone and nobody had a big celebration. How could we? Nobody had known how old she was, and even if we had, Sylvia would not have liked a big fuss made over her. Still, her death had been unexpected. At least *I* had been unprepared, since I had been convinced that she would live forever.

The phone rang in my office, a room that seemed terribly cramped and quiet since I had come home from Minnesota. I used to think it was cozy and quaint. Now only the hum of the soda machine could be heard in this ancient two-story house. I answered, "This is Torie."

"It's your mother."

"Hi, Mom. What's up?"

"I made fried chicken. Too much even for Colin to eat. You and Rudy and the kids want to come by and eat dinner with us?"

"No, I don't think so," I said.

"Tor-ie," she said in her best motherly voice. "You're not hungry? You're always hungry. Especially for food you don't have to cook."

"Haven't been hungry in weeks," I said, ignoring the last remark.

"You're depressed."

"I'm not depressed," I said. "I'm just . . ."

"Yes?"

"Distracted. And . . . and busy. Do you know how much stuff has to be done here? Way too much to take time out to eat," I said. Which was a lie. Normally I could eat at any time, any place. I'd just order a pizza, eat, and do my work. But since I had watched them put Sylvia in the ground . . . Well, I'm just not hungry.

"Distracted, my butt," Mom said.

"I'll send Rudy and the kids over to eat. I wouldn't have time anyway."

"If I may be so bold," my mother said.

"I thought that was my line. You're never bold. You're always the perfect lady."

"You need some help going through Sylvia's belongings," she said. "Why don't you call somebody to help you?"

"I don't need help."

"And Rudy won't stop and ask for directions," she said. "That's how frustrating it is watching you do this by yourself. I know you need help, but you just won't stop and ask for directions."

"Mom—"

"Get some help."

"Who? Helen has her own business to run, Charity's babysitting her brother's twins, Collette is busy with her own career—everybody I can think of is too busy," I said.

"How about your sister?"

I hadn't thought of that. Stephanie had found out she was pregnant and decided to take a leave of absence from her teaching job. Maybe she would be available for a few weeks. "I'll call her."

"Good," she said. "You shouldn't be in that stuffy home all by yourself."

"Yeah, yeah, yeah, whatever." I guess she was proof that once a mother, always a mother. I actually found a bit of joy in that thought. I would get to drive my children crazy until I was old and shuffled off this mortal coil. Something to look forward to.

3

"I'll send home leftovers with Rudy."

"Sure," I said.

We said our good-byes, and I hung up the phone and fingered the postcard in my hand. It was addressed to Sylvia, but there were no words on the postcard other than *I think you have forgotten your promise.*

No signature. Nothing. Just those seven words. I couldn't explain why that bothered me so much. I couldn't help but think about what the promise could have been and why she hadn't kept it. Or maybe she had kept the promise once she received this gentle reminder. Had this postcard made her spring into action? Or had she just left the promise unfulfilled?

I found it difficult to believe that Sylvia would not have kept her word.

Sylvia was a hateful, cantankerous spitfire, but she was an honorable person. Maybe that's why this bothered me so much. I didn't want to believe that Sylvia hadn't kept her word. And there was nobody to ask about this mystery. Her sister, Wilma, had died about two years ago, and her brother had died years and years ago. The only people left would have been her brother's descendants and most of them were entirely too angry at the fact she didn't leave them anything in her will to speak to me.

So I supposed I would never know. And for me, that's just not acceptable. There are tons of things that I don't know in this world, but I am unaware that I don't know them, and therefore don't care. But this—well, this would drive me crazy.

To make matters worse, the image on the front of the postcard was of a small child, about three or four years old, dressed in a tattered winter coat, striped leggings, and shoes with a big hole in the toe of the left one. I assumed the child was a girl because of the leggings and the hat—and the fact that she had a doll, with only one eye, tucked under her arm. The girl stared back at the photographer with contempt and . . . defiance.

I stood and stretched, grabbed some change out of a bowl on my desk, and stepped into the hallway for a soda. I automatically looked to my right, nearly expecting to see Sylvia standing in the kitchen, steeping tea. She wasn't there, of course. She would never be there. I was surprised by how much I missed her. Or maybe it was guilt. All those times I spewed venom about her, and here she left me the Gaheimer House, everything in it, three hundred thousand in cash plus a life insurance policy, and several homes throughout town and even out of town.

The Dr Pepper was sitting in the bottom of the machine, waiting for me to pick it up. I didn't remember hearing it drop. I went back to my office with the soda in hand and picked up the phone and dialed my sister.

"Hey, Steph," I said, popping the can open. "It's Torie. I've got a proposition for you."

TWO

New Kassel, Missouri, is my favorite place in the whole world. All that I hold dear resides within its boundaries. It's hard to explain, really, but for me, New Kassel is almost a person. She has her own personality, her own moods, her own rhythms, and definitely her own voice. She speaks to me quite often. I love the Mississippi that rolls along and, for the most part, gently caresses the edges of town. The Mississippi can, however, remind us who's boss, and has on a few occasions. From my bedroom window I can see the tugboats and barges coming and going along the river. I wait eagerly every spring for the lilacs to come into bloom, and for Tobias Thorley's prizewinning roses to make an appearance every June.

I walked along River Pointe Road and entered the Lick-a-Pot Candy Shoppe, where Helen Wickland—another lifelong resident—was scoring her latest batch of fudge. The smell of sugar was so heavy it made my mouth water. I felt like an experiment by that Pavlov guy.

"What kind did you make?" I asked.

Helen looked up and over the rim of her glasses. "Torie, hey," she said. "Peanut butter."

"Oooh, give me a pound," I said. It sounded good. It smelled good. Now, if only I could remember to actually eat it.

"You look like you're losing some weight," Helen said.

"Really?" I asked and looked down at myself. "Burning the candle at both ends."

"A lot to do?" she said and gestured in the general direction of the Gaheimer House.

"Tons," I said.

Helen was a decade or so older than I was, with heavily frosted short hair and a pleasant smile. She was usually the person who filled in for me at the Gaheimer House and, indeed, had been doing my tours when Sylvia died.

"Maybe when I get this fudge done for the Strawberry Festival, I can help," she said.

"Oh, no," I said. "My sister's coming down to help for a while."

"Well, that's good," she said.

"Actually, I was here to talk to you about the Strawberry Festival," I said.

"Oh, sure," she said, and wiped her hands on a towel sitting on the counter.

"You've got somebody to run the store those weekends, right?"

"Yes," she said. "Scott's going to forgo the car show up in St. Charles and man the store."

"So, I can count on you at booth number four on Saturday from seven to three and"—I fished a piece of paper out of my pants pocket—"and booth number two on Sunday from noon to four."

"That's right," she said.

"Great," I said.

"Have you inspected this year's batch yet?" Helen asked.

"Not yet," I said. "I'm on my way over there now."

"I hear it's the best yet," Helen said.

"Good," I said. "I'll talk to you later."

"Torie, are you all right?" Helen asked.

"Fine. Just tired," I said and started to go.

"Oh, you forgot your fudge," Helen said, laying the slab on the counter. She went to the cash register and punched in some numbers. "It's—"

I handed her a twenty. "Keep the change."

It was June in New Kassel. Quite frankly, May, June, and October are the best months in central Missouri. May and June are warm but not too humid, ànd everything is green. The past few years have been really dry, so by the time July gets here, the trees and grass are turning brown. But June—well, June is warm, green, and lush. I walked along, making the turns where I needed to, without really paying attention to what street I was on. I didn't need to. I knew the town that well. Within a few minutes, I found myself at Virginia Burgermeister's door.

I knocked and waited. A round, gregarious, pink woman answered the door, wearing a chartreuse apron over a very old peach paisley dress. Close to seventy, Virgie Burgermeister, the mother-in-law of Charity Burgermeister, was one of the nicest people in the world. Her cooking could rival even my mother's.

She was our Head Jam Maker. In this town, that was a very important title.

"Virgie, good to see you," I said.

"Come on in, Torie." She swung the door open. "I was expectin' you to come by soon. You wanna taste this year's batch?"

"I can't wait."

I walked through her small and very claustrophobic two-bedroom house. Much of the claustrophobia was due to the gold shag carpeting on the living room walls. True, it made the house quite soundproof, and it hadn't kept her from hanging a large gilt mirror on one wall and a family portrait on the other. But walls should not be furry.

The kitchen, thank goodness, was not furry. Down the steps and into the basement we went. There I was greeted with what seemed like a thousand pressure cookers, four stoves, and a million jars of strawberry jam. This year's batch. Okay, maybe not a million jars, but damn, it was a lot of jam.

"Pick a jar," she said with a wave of her arm, like one of those six-foot-tall models on *The Price Is Right*. She smiled brightly at all of this year's hard work.

I walked over and picked a jar at random, opened it, and looked around for a spoon, which she miraculously produced from thin air. I tasted it, and it was delicious. Just tart enough, but with lots of sweet to go with it. Smooth and fruity.

"Now try the preserves," she said and pointed to a small stack in the corner. She never made as much preserves as she did jam. I tried a jar of preserves, and it tasted very much like the jam, only with chunks of fruit in it.

"And the jelly?" I asked.

Virgie gave me a disgruntled look. "I'm afraid Krista had to do the jelly. My jelly-making fingers just weren't workin' this year."

"Oh," I said, wondering how different her jelly-making fingers were from her jam-making fingers. "Well, I'm sure that's fine."

Why hadn't I known Krista was making the jelly? It wasn't like me to miss out on that kind of detail.

"Delia made fifty pies, I heard," she said.

"Good," I said. "Are those to sell or for the pie-eating contest?"

"Delia would not waste her time on pies somebody was going to shove their face into. No, those pies were made by Mrs. Castlereagh."

The mayor's wife.

"All right," I said. "Well, it looks like everything's ready to go. Bands will be here on time. Booths have people to work them. I'll see you all this weekend."

"Here," Virgie said. She handed me the open jars of jam and preserves and then handed me two more of each, unopened. "You look like you're losin' weight."

"So I've been told," I said.

I headed up the steps, with Virgie close behind. When we were at the top of the stairs, she retrieved the jars from me long enough to put them in a plastic bag. "Rudy coming by the usual time to load up the jars?"

"He should be by with the truck about five in the morning on Saturday."

"Good," she said. "Take care now."

"Right," I said and was escorted out the door.

•

By the time I arrived home I was weighted down with fudge, jam, preserves, and a half dozen of Tobias's prizewinning roses. Before I could open the door, Rudy opened it for me. "Hi, honey!" He smiled and hugged me while I still stood on the threshold.

"What did you do?" I asked. Normally he stays snug in his re-cliner. He never meets me at the door.

"I didn't do a blasted thing, for once," he said.

"What did the kids do?"

"Well . . ." he said and ushered me inside. "Nothing, really. I mean, Rachel passed out at band camp, but since some cute trumpet player caught her it isn't nearly as much of a tragedy as it would have been."

"What? Is she okay?"

"She's fine. In fact, since the cute trumpet player caught her, I think she's considering passing out tomorrow, too."

"Oh, great."

Rudy continued. "Mary filled Tobias's garden with coffee grounds because she thought it would help his flowers grow—" Rudy looked down at the roses in my hand.

"I guess he's unaware of it so far," I said.

"She meant well."

"Where'd she get all the coffee?"

"Well, she took ours and then asked for donations all over town. Turned out she got like fifteen pounds of coffee total."

"Great," I said. I was seriously worried about a town of people who would give coffee to a third grader just because she asked for it.

"But, really, that was nothing," he said and shrugged his shoul-ders.

I stared at him. "Are you feeling all right?"

"I'm fine," he said.

"You forgot one."

"Huh?"

"Our son?"

"Oh, Matthew . . . well, it was nothing overly gross."

Rudy didn't volunteer any more than that, and frankly I was too tired to care, so I let it go. I put my things down on the kitchen table and rubbed my face with my hands. I was so exhausted. "I'm going to take a shower and go to bed."

"Go to bed? Honey, it's . . . seven-thirty."

"So?"

"So you're the woman who burns the candle at both ends."

"Well, my candle just met in the middle and burned me. I'm tired," I said.

Rudy fidgeted with the edge on his pockets. Something was up. I said, "Okay, I don't have time for a bunch of crap, so just tell me what you did so I can berate you and go to bed."

"I didn't do anything," he said, gesturing to himself with both hands.

The hair prickled on the back of my neck. "All right, what's going on?"

"Well . . ." he said, "my mother is coming to town."

"Oh," I said. That wasn't so bad. Dinner with her once, maybe a trip to the park for a picnic, and she'd be back to sunny California. As long as there were plenty of other people around at these gatherings, I could live with that. "Great. I'm going to bed now."

"She hasn't been in town in three years and that's all you can say?"

"That's wonderful, Rudy. What do you want me to say?"

"The woman lives over a thousand miles away."

"What? You want me to give her a parade? She chose to move to southern California. Why is this such a big deal? I'm happy for you. We'll have a nice visit, you'll actually get to see your sister, who only lives thirty miles away, and all will be well. I'm going to bed."

"She's staying here."

I turned deliberately, ever so slowly, so as not to give myself whiplash. "I'm sorry, but I thought you just said something incredibly stupid."

"She's staying with us."

"Oh, no, she's not. She's staying with Amy. Like she always does."

"There is no *always*," he said. "She's only been here three times in nine years."

I wasn't sure what his point was, but I kept my silence, afraid that I might actually bark at him if I tried to speak.

"My sister is out of town."

"Oh, good God!" I yelled. Couldn't help it.

"Torie—"

"There are such things as hotels, you know."

"She's my mother," he said.

"She's Cruella De Vil!"

"Torie!" he snapped.

"I cannot believe you would do this. All the things I've got going on right now . . . I do not—*not*—need this."

"She'll be good, I promise," he said.

"You know, Rudy, if you have to promise your mother will be good, she will not be good! What does that say? You have to vouch for the behavior of your mother!"

"She's still my mother," he said. "She has the right to stay here."

"You didn't ask me!" I yelled.

"You would have said no," he said. The veins in his neck began to protrude, like big nightcrawlers beneath his skin.

"You're damn right I would have said no! What is the matter with you?" I screeched.

By this time the children had gathered in the hall, because although Rudy and I disagreed quite often, we rarely screamed at one another.

"What's the matter?" Mary asked.

"Grandma O is coming," Rachel said.

"Oh," Mary said, as if that explained it all. "She hates Mother."

Rachel picked Matthew up, and all three headed back down the hallway to their rooms.

Their interruption gave me a few seconds to calm down, although just barely. "Look," I said through clenched teeth, "there's only one person in this world who hates me more than your mother, and that's the mayor. But only on good days. And I would never invite him to stay in my home."

"My mother does not hate you."

"Your mother hates me. Do you remember the first time I met her? Do you? She called me mountain folk. Remember that? Mountain folk. Or do you have that same disease she does and you conveniently forget when she's been an ass?"

"You're my wife," he said and tried to hug me.

"Which is why she hates me," I said, shaking his arm off. "Look, Rudy, I can't deal with this right now. I'll go stay with my mother."

"You can't go stay with your mother. How would that look?"

"Who cares what it looks like? It didn't bother your mother what it looked like when she told all our wedding guests that our marriage wouldn't last. All of them, Rudy. Even my family."

"She's apologized for that."

"Oh, she's a regular Gandhi."

"It would look really bad, Torie, if you went to stay with your mother, and you know it."

"Well, it would look even worse if I stayed here and killed her. Just think what that would do to our positions in this town. Me in jail, wearing stripes and . . . and tracing all the family trees of the inmates for favors. You an outcast from your bowling team. Really, I think I should go stay with my mother."

"You know, I let your mother live with us," he said. "The least you can do is play hostess to mine for a few weeks."

"My mother likes you. My mother doesn't tell you what a terrible person you are because you have lint balls on your socks. My mother doesn't ask you how much money you make every time she sees you. My *mother* . . . wait, did you say a few weeks?"

He shrugged. "Maybe a month."

I was going to have a stroke. Which was actually good. Because then I'd be dead and I wouldn't have to worry about killing my mother-in-law.

"You—" I said, pointing my finger at him. I stopped short of calling him any of the names I had on the tip of my tongue. He was my husband, after all, so I had to be careful just what names I did call him. Anything dealing with genetics would be bad, because we had children together. Still, I had to say something. "Slimebucket!"

"Torie! She's my mother, she's coming to stay, and that's all there is to it."

"Hmmm," I said. "How did this happen, Rudy? Somewhere in that conversation with your mother it never occurred to you that this would be a bad idea? Or could you just not tell her no?"

That was it. I nailed it. He knew it was a bad idea. He knew his mother couldn't behave. He knew I'd be upset. But he just couldn't tell her no. His eyes told me the whole story. It was funny, though, the fact that he considered himself guilt free in all of this. His mother insisted she come and stay with us, so how could that be his fault? Right?

I was so angry, I couldn't speak, couldn't cry, couldn't do anything but clench my teeth and fists and stomp up the stairs. Throwing myself on the bed, I breathed deeply for a few moments, feeling the poison in my body ebb—the poison that my body seems to make when I argue with my husband. I was going to go to sleep and never wake up. I was just going to hit that snooze button of life until I was eighty and there was no sign of my mother-in-law and the coast was clear. Then I'd get up.

Well, there was one good thing about the fight with Rudy and the disastrous news of my mother-in-law's impending visit. I had forgotten about that blasted postcard.

THE NEW KASSEL GAZETTE
The News You Might Miss
by Eleanore Murdoch

It's Strawberry Time! This is the time of year when people come from miles around to trample our lawns, defile our bathrooms, and write graffiti on the bridge. But that's all right. We make more than enough money to clean it all up and have some left over. And we won't see this much traffic again until the Pickin' and Grinnin' Festival. So everybody be nice to those tourists!

The New Kassel school marching band is holding a car wash next Sunday to raise money for their new band uniforms. I've seen the cars in this town. Some of you haven't washed your cars in a month. Or since last fall. So put your money to good use, and you won't be so ashamed when you drive around town!

Also, there's a meeting at the historical society this Wednesday. We'll be voting on officers. I feel a change blowing in the wind.

Until next time,
Eleanore

Three

I knew I was dreaming, but I couldn't wake myself up. Sylvia was standing in the kitchen of the Gaheimer House steeping her tea, as I had seen her do a thousand and one times. Her silvery-white hair hung down loose to the backs of her knees. In life, she had always worn her hair in two braids wrapped around her head. In her casket, however, in death, her hair had been down long, brushed until it shined and lying elegantly over one shoulder.

I know, because I had been the one to style it.

She would probably hate me for that. Somewhere up in heaven or wherever it was that she now resided, she was ticked off because I sent her into the afterworld with her hair down. It wouldn't be the first time she was angry with me. But it would definitely be the last.

In my dream she turned around and smiled at me. A smile. I was definitely dreaming. She took my hand in hers. "There's much to be done," she said. Her hand was warm to the touch; her smile denoted a certain understanding. I stood riveted, unable to move away from her.

Somewhere in the distance I heard my name being called. I glanced over my shoulder to find all of my family standing behind me, except my mother, who was sitting in her wheelchair. And the more I looked, the more people I saw. Half the town was there, crammed into the hall with the soda machine. "Torie, come on," my mother said. They all nodded their heads and beckoned to me. *Yes, come with us.*

"There is much to be done," Sylvia repeated. When I turned back to look at her, the teacup fell to the floor and splashed tea all over my legs. Sylvia's grip on my hand tightened.

"Torie, as your mother, I'm telling you to come with us!" My mother's voice rang out like a warning bell, but I couldn't move. I couldn't take my eyes off of Sylvia's ancient and cracked face.

"So much left undone," Sylvia said.

"Why me?" I asked. "Why did you leave everything to me? Why?"

"Torie, let's go!" I heard my mother's voice, demanding and parental.

Suddenly Sylvia's grip grew too tight. Those warm fingers turned to ice. Soft and smooth skin turned rough and purple. My fingers ached. My bones were being crushed.

Then I heard a voice behind me. An irritatingly nasal, singsongy voice. The type of voice that had the perpetual effect of nails on a chalkboard. "Oh, for crying out loud, Torie. Quit being such a ninny and get over here where your family needs you."

It was the voice of my mother-in-law.

Sylvia's face looked confused for a moment. Clearly she had not expected to have her thunder stolen from her. I turned around to see Mrs. O'Shea, a thin, wiry little woman, with nearly white hair and vacant gray eyes. The devil's spawn. The woman responsible for all my ulcers and nearly every panic attack I've ever had. She shoved her way forward through the crowd of people. Both hands were on her hips, and her body language spoke volumes of irritation.

"I knew he shouldn't have married you. I raised him to be a good Catholic boy. He was going to be a lawyer. He was going to go to Harvard. And then *you* came along and ruined everything. Now get your butt over here. He needs you now. You will not abandon your family. Come on, what are you waiting for? Huh? Eat too much fudge for Christmas? Middle age making you lazy? Good God, girl, when was the last time you dyed your hair?"

"All right!" I said. "I'm coming. Just shut up! Please."

"Torie, Torie. Wake up."

"Just shut up! Please."

"Torie, it's me, Rudy. Wake up."

I was awake. Somehow I had managed to bring myself out of my nightmare only to plop myself smack dab in the middle of reality. I wasn't sure which was worse. I stared up at Rudy's brown eyes and for a brief moment was happy to see him. Then I remembered that he'd told his mother she could stay *in our house* for a month. "Get away from me," I said.

"You were having a dream," he said.

"A nightmare," I said. "Your mother was the star."

"Still angry, huh?"

I pushed the blankets off of me, a little surprised to see that it was daylight. I had slept in my clothes. Hadn't even brushed my teeth the night before. I had fallen asleep exactly as I had dropped onto the bed after my argument with Rudy. "Still angry? Rudy, you'll be lucky if I'm ever nice to you again."

"It's not that bad," he began.

I held up my hand. "I don't want to talk about this. Not now, not later, not ever. Don't speak to me."

To give him credit, Rudy really did look as though I'd struck him. Which was exactly what I had wanted. If I had to be miserable because his mother was here, then he'd have to be miserable, too. It was his fault, after all.

I locked myself in the bathroom and took a shower. When I was finished and dressed, Rudy was gone. The kids were downstairs watching cartoons, waiting for breakfast, which I made for them. After an hour of overseeing everybody getting dressed, groomed, and out the door, I dropped Rachel off at band camp and went to the Gaheimer House with Mary and Matthew.

I still couldn't quite shake the cloud of the dream, though. I half expected to find dried tea on the floor of the kitchen. Of course, there wasn't any. I gave the kids some paper to shred—yes, that really does keep them busy—and got myself a Dr Pepper. I took a big, cold drink and was happy that there was still something in life that was exactly as it should be. If all else went crazy, at least there was some solace in the fact that Dr Pepper would never change.

Now, if some corporate schmuck decides to change Dr Pepper, well, I won't be responsible for my actions.

An hour later I had decided that if Sylvia appeared in my office alive and well, I'd kill her. The woman had kept every receipt since 1920. She'd kept every warranty, every manual to every appliance. It was as if it were a matter of national security that she know how to properly work a toaster that was made in 1958, even though she'd had two upgrades since then—and kept their manuals as well. I had three huge boxes of receipts and stuff to shred and then toss, and I hadn't even made a dent in the majority of the paperwork in this house.

"Oh, Matthew, honey. Don't eat the paper," I said.

My two-year-old looked up at me with a surprised expression, as if he didn't understand what I was saying. "I know it's tough when you find out you shouldn't eat things that obviously taste good," I said. He gave me a toothy grin and shrieked.

"Mom," Mary asked, "why did Sylvia die?"

"Because she was old," I said.

"Are you old?"

"Not that old," I said. "Older than you."

"Oh, that's a relief," she sighed.

Obviously she had been worried about me kicking the bucket.

"Mom?"

"Yes?"

"Why does Grandma O hate you?"

I shrugged. "She's a very . . . Oh, I don't want to talk about it."

"I think it's funny when she rolls her eyes at you," she said.

"Really," I said. "Well, I'm glad you can find something to be happy about."

"She smells good," Mary said.

"Yes, she does," I said. There. I said something nice about her.

"Mom?"

"What?"

"Can I have a cat?"

"No."

There was a knock at the door, interrupting our usual routine of questions and answers. The Gaheimer House had been closed for tours until further notice. There was a sign on the front window that said so. Most of the townspeople would come to the back door, so I was confused as I headed through the hall and the elaborately decorated front sitting room in which the marble floors were dusty. Sylvia would kill me if she knew that. Maybe that was what she was trying to tell me in the dream. I needed to mop and shine the floors.

I opened the door to find Deputy Edwin Duran standing there looking at me with his piercing blue eyes. In high school he had been the quarterback for Meyersville, another small town about five miles south of New Kassel. "Hey, how are you?" I asked.

"Pretty good," he said. I opened the door wider for him to enter and he did, removing his hat as he crossed the threshold. "Sorry it's taken me so long."

I was confused. I didn't remember asking him for any favors recently. "What are you talking about?"

It was his turn to look equally confused. "Oh, well, I assumed Sylvia had told you."

"How can she tell me anything? She's dead."

"I mean, before she died. Or in her will or instructions or something." His expression owed as much to surprise as it did embarrassment.

"I don't know what you're talking about," I said.

"The house," he said and leaned in as if somebody might overhear. "My house."

"What about it?"

"Sylvia owned the title," he said. "I told her, oh, the night before she died that I would bring the rent check by, and it just slipped my mind. Here."

Deputy Duran handed me a check for two months' worth of rent. At least I assumed it was two months' worth, because it was a rather large sum and in the comment line he'd written "for June and July."

"Oh," I said.

"So I guess I just pay you now, right?"

"Right," I said.

Oh, jeez. It hadn't really registered that I was a landlady now, too. It made sense. All those houses Sylvia owned and left to me had people living in them. It takes me a while sometimes, but eventually I catch on.

"You seem surprised," he said.

"Well, I haven't gotten around to grasping the fact that I'm a landlady," I said.

"That's okay."

"Do you need anything? Faucets working okay?"

He smiled. "Everything's fine."

"You need a paint job or something?"

"I don't need anything," he said.

"Gosh, I don't even know when your rent is due," I said.

"It's due the first," he said. "Sylvia was so distracted that night when I talked to her. She usually wrote it down when somebody was late on the rent, and the day they'd pay her, so she could keep track. I guess she just forgot to write it down."

Not that I would have understood her notes. "Distracted?" I asked.

"Yeah, that's the whole reason I was out here. I got called out."

"You mean Sylvia dialed 911?"

"No, she just called me direct. She did that every now and then. You know, I did a lot of favors for her. All the time, in fact. That night she called and said she had heard a prowler."

"A prowler?"

"Yeah, she was concerned that her security system wasn't working right," he said. "But I checked everything out. Even the video. It all seemed to be in working order."

The surveillance cameras had temporarily slipped my mind.

Sylvia had them installed about a year ago. I'd often wondered why she hadn't done it sooner. Not only did the Gaheimer House hold a veritable fortune in antiques, but Sylvia also had lived here. Maybe before then she'd never felt the need, since her sister, Wilma, had lived here, too. Security in numbers. At any rate, the cameras only watched the outside of the house. Nothing inside.

"So anyway, I checked the video and the alarms, and everything seemed fine. She still seemed distracted, though. But I guess when you're that old and worth that much money . . ."

His voice trailed off, and he shuffled his feet. Money. Now I was worth *that much money*. It made him uncomfortable. Rudy and I had been his equals just a few weeks ago, and even though I hadn't changed one iota, he assumed I had.

"All she said was she heard a prowler?"

"Yeah," he replied. "One thing was strange, though."

"What's that?"

"By the time I got back to the station in Wisteria, she had called again. That time she spoke to Miller and said she wanted to talk to one of us the next day. The next day she was dead." He shrugged.

I said nothing.

"You know, she was an old battle-ax, but when I dislocated my shoulder that one time and was off from work, she let my rent slide for three months and told me not to worry about paying her," he said. "And when Leigh lost the last baby, she sent flowers."

"Well, that was nice," I said.

"Yeah, but she sent them before we'd told anybody. How'd she know that kinda stuff?"

"I don't know," I said. "She had spies everywhere."

"I believe it," he said. "All right, well, I'm off to work. Got the day shift today."

"All right," I said. "Let me know if you need anything."

"I will," he said.

I shut the door and stared at the check in my hand. A thousand bucks. And the mortgage on his little two-bedroom bungalow was paid off. I went from never knowing how I was going to pay all the bills to suddenly having more money than I knew what to do with. Everybody in town knew it, too.

I tapped my lip with the edge of his check and wondered. I wondered about the prowler Sylvia had the night before she died. Obviously, if none of the alarms had been tripped, it had been her imagination. Still, it bothered me. She had been an old lady, all by herself. I had been in Minnesota. And why had she called the sheriff's station and asked to speak to somebody the next day?

The next day when she had been found dead by Helen Wickland.

I wandered back into my office. Matthew was throwing paper everywhere, and Mary was giggling at him, a contagious giggle that showed the sheer joy she was sharing with him. I smiled at them. "Mom?" she said.

"Mary?"

"What?" she asked.

"If I'm the only mother in the room, why do you have to start every sentence with 'Mom'?"

She shrugged. "Mom?"

"Yes?" I sighed.

"Every little kid should have a cat, you know."

Four

Two hours later I was seated in my favorite booth at Fräulein Krista's Speisehaus eating lunch with Mary and Matthew. Fräulein Krista's is our little Bavarian gem stuck in the middle of midwestern America. The waiters all wear velvet knickers, and the waitresses all wear dirndl skirts, and the whole place has the general feel of an inn deep in the Black Forest. Even Fräulein Krista resembled a character from the Brothers Grimm, with her yellow-blond hair, blue eyes, and long legs.

At the end of the bar sat the stuffed grizzly bear that the townsfolk had nicknamed Sylvia. Sylvia, the big ferocious bear.

"Mom?"

"Yes, Mary?"

"How long are you going to be mad at Dad?"

"If he's lucky, just until he's dead."

She giggled into her soda cup. That's the great thing about my kids, they understand my sense of humor. Some kids would have been horrified by that remark, but not mine. The sad part was, at that moment, it wasn't a joke at all. I'd meant it.

"Mom?"

"Yes?"

"What exactly is a slimebucket?"

"It's a slimy bucket."

"Mom?"

"Oh, my God, Mary. You have to stop saying 'Mom' or I am going to scream."

A rotten grin spread across her angelic face, and her green eyes sparkled like crackling jade. "Mom?"

"You are not funny."

"Do I have to eat all of my food?"

"Of course you do," I said.

"Why?"

"Why do you think?" I asked.

"Because there's starving children in Africa?"

"Exactly," I said.

"Why don't they just move?"

"What?"

"If they're always starving in Africa, why don't they move to . . . I don't know, Australia or something? Then they won't be hungry. And I won't have to eat all my food."

"You are killing me," I said.

Just then Sheriff Colin Brooke came walking into the restaurant. He always seemed to know when I was there. Of course, his being married to my mother might have had something to do with that. She still had her old network of spies from when I was a teenager. My mother was proof that you didn't need expensive equipment and a badge to know exactly what was going on in a small town.

"Hey, Torie," he said and squeezed himself into the booth next to Mary. I say "squeezed" because he had a very large frame and being married to my mother—the greatest cook in the world—had done a lot to flesh that frame out.

"Paw-Paw Badge," Matthew said. For some reason, Colin is known as "Grandpa with the Badge," like some sort of Native American name. Colin won't admit it, but he likes this immensely.

"How you guys doin'?" He stole a french fry from Mary.

"Fine," I said. It is disturbing beyond belief to know that I cannot eat lunch in this town without being interrupted.

"I hear your mother-in-law's coming to visit," he said.

"How did you know about that?"

"Your mother told me."

"How did Mom find out? I haven't talked to her."

"Rudy called her and asked her to talk some sense into you," he said.

"Oh," I said.

"How's things going over at the house?" he asked.

"The Gaheimer House, you mean?"

"Yeah."

"Okay. Stephanie is coming to help, but not until tomorrow."

"Things'll work out," he said.

"What is that supposed to mean?"

"Just, you know. Things might seem . . . bleak now, but it'll get better," he said.

He was actually trying to make me feel better. It was sweet. Wonder what my mother bribed him with? "Can I ask you a question?" I asked.

"Yes," he said and plopped another fry into his mouth.

"Have you read the reports on Sylvia's death?"

Colin stopped chewing and stared at me. His eyes narrowed, and then they widened, and then he sighed with exasperation and pinched the bridge of his nose with his right hand. "You are a piece of work." He swallowed the fry. "She was a hundred and two years old."

"What has her age got to do with anything?"

"She was old. Her body was tired. She stopped breathing. End of story," he said.

"And the end of her," Mary added.

Colin and I both stared at her. She shrugged and took a bite of her chicken. Matthew took that moment to squish his mashed potatoes between his fingers. "Matthew!" I said and held up his hand.

Colin handed me a napkin, and I wiped Matthew's hand. "Don't play with your food."

"Cats play with their food," Mary said.

"All the more reason not to get one. It'll be a bad influence on your brother," I said.

"Mary wants a cat?" Colin asked.

"Yeah," Mary answered and gave him the big Mommy-is-being-mean eyes.

"What kind?" he asked.

"I'd like one of those patchy-looking ones," Mary said, smiling up at him. See? If she looks sweet enough, Grandpa with the Badge will buy her a cat and the hell with what her mother says. My daughter is a con artist.

"Oh, a calico," he said.

"She's not getting a cat!" I said. "Don't encourage her."

"Ah, come on. It's just a cat," Colin said. Great, that was all I needed, the man with the badge to take Mary's side. There'd be no living with her.

"We have a dog," I said.

"So?" he asked. "What's a dog have to do with a cat?"

"Can we forget about the cat?" I said.

"I'm going to name it Patches," Mary said and batted her lashes.

"Aw," Colin said and gave me that look that said I was a hardened criminal and a terrible mother. "She's already got a name picked out for it."

"Colin!"

"Yes, Torie, I read the report," he said.

"And?"

"What do you expect? You expect that there was a smoking gun lying on the bed and I'm just ignoring it?"

"No, Colin," I said. "It's just that it's weird that she'd call somebody out because she thought she heard a prowler. In fact, she called *twice*, and then she was dead the next day. Don't you think that's weird?"

"Not when the victim is a hundred and two years old!" he said. "Why can't you accept the fact that Sylvia was old and just died?"

"Because this was Sylvia. She was supposed to live forever."

"Well, the powers that be had other plans," he said.

"I still think . . ."

"What? She would have told you she was about to die? Is that it?"

"No," I said, looking around the room for no particular reason other than to hide my discomfort. "I just think if somebody called about a prowler and was dead the next day, somebody would have done an autopsy or something."

"Well, you are the executor of her will. Why didn't you order an autopsy?" he asked.

"Because I didn't know about the whole prowler thing until this morning," I said. "Otherwise, I would have."

"Well, if you can convince a judge that there's reason enough, we can exhume the body and do an autopsy. Is that what you want, Torie? You want to exhume the body?"

"No," I said, staring at my half-eaten salad.

"Then what do you want?" he asked.

"Mom, how do you resume a body?" Mary asked.

We both ignored her.

"I just wish you had thought of it. You knew about the prowler," I said.

"If it makes you feel better to blame me, then go ahead," he said.

"No, that's not it."

"Look, she was a hundred and two years old. She just died. I saw nothing in the report to make me think anybody other than Sylvia had been in that house all night. The alarms were never tripped, doors and windows locked. I did not order an autopsy because there was nothing to indicate that I needed to order one."

I crossed my arms. "Whatever," I said. I always got angry when my girls gave me the crossed-arm-whatever, because that meant they didn't have anything intelligent to say. I guess I didn't have anything intelligent to say.

"You can read the report if you want," he said.

"Did you ask Helen if she saw anything?" I asked.

"She saw Sylvia. Dead," he said.

"Mom, were her eyes open or closed when Helen found her?" Mary asked.

"It doesn't matter," I said.

"Well, if they were closed, then she was sleeping, which is better. Because then she wouldn't have been afraid," Mary said.

I stared at Colin across the table and across the plates of food. Then I looked away because tears had pooled in my eyes. I didn't want to think about Sylvia being alone and being afraid. "Look, I'm not saying there was any foul play," I said. "I'm just saying that there might have been more to it."

"Which means foul play," he said and laughed. "Torie, you really *are* a piece of work."

"Thank you very much," I said. I opened my purse to pay for our lunch. Colin pointed at something sticking out of my purse.

"What's that?" he asked.

"Oh," I said. "It's a postcard. Found it in Sylvia's things."

"Of all the stuff in that house, this is the thing you keep with you?"

I shrugged. "Can't help it. I can't forget about it."

He plucked it from my purse and looked at the front of it. Then he flipped it over and read the back. "What's the promise?" he asked.

"I don't know," I said. "It's driving me crazy."

"Well, take it easy, Torie. All right? Let Rudy's mother do some work around your house. Take a load off of you. Let her cook a meal or two. All right?" He handed the postcard back to me.

I rolled my eyes.

"Grandma O always rolls her eyes at Mom, too," Mary chimed in.

Five

I ate my dinner mostly in silence. Yes, I was pouting, but it wouldn't have mattered. Rachel never stopped talking about these two unbelievably cute brothers in marching band. How one would say this, and the other would say that, and just when she'd come to a conclusion on which one was the cutest, she'd blush and change her mind. Her brain had turned as sticky as our macaroni and cheese.

Rudy, of course, was seriously disturbed about Rachel's new-found interest in the opposite sex. She'd always liked boys, but now that she was in junior high, well, I felt like we were guest stars on one of those teen sitcoms. And just think, we had all of high school left to go through.

"So what instrument do these brothers play?" Rudy asked, obviously irritated.

"Instruments?" Rachel said. "Oh, yeah. Uh . . . I think trumpets."

"You think?" he asked.

"Well, I didn't pay much attention to the instruments."

"Okay," I said, and stood up. "I'm going to the Gaheimer House."

"What?" Rudy asked. "You don't work in the evenings."

"Well, I do today. Didn't get a whole lot done with the kids there earlier, so you can watch them. Have fun." I put my plate in the sink.

"My mother will be here Saturday morning," he said.

"That's nice, dear," I said. I kissed each one of the kids on the head, gave them all instructions for the rest of the night, grabbed my purse, and walked out the door. Since I didn't have the kids to haul around, I walked the few blocks down to the Gaheimer House.

The truth of the matter was that the postcard was driving me nuts. It was like this little hot ember burning a hole in me. I had to find out something more about it. I'd be happy if I could figure out who the little girl was. I got in the house, turned off the alarms, and went to my office. I switched on the light and found my magnifying glass in one of the drawers. Then I took the postcard out and studied the back of it. The date was the eighth of something, 1930. It was postmarked from . . . The state was definitely Iowa. I had figured that out before. It was the city that I couldn't make out. I squinted my eyes, as if that would help. One word. Something and then a "que."

I got out my road atlas and turned to the page for Iowa. I scanned the map quickly, and the first town that jumped out at me was Dubuque. Seven letters. I looked back at the postcard. The word had seven letters. The first letter could have been an O, but I had been thinking all along it was a D. Now I was almost positive it was Dubuque.

I didn't remember Sylvia ever talking about Iowa, much less Dubuque, about having been there or having family there. In fact, I wasn't at all sure Sylvia had ever left Missouri. I slumped back in my chair and twirled the magnifying glass in my hand.

I turned the postcard over and studied the photograph for the fiftieth time since having found the blasted thing, only this time I used my magnifying glass. The background was sort of desolate, not a lot going on, just some empty space with buildings on the right-hand side and something big and dark on the left. A person stood in the distance, but other than that it was a person, I couldn't make a whole lot out. The girl held the doll, but this time I noticed she had something clutched in the other hand. I couldn't tell what it was.

I booted up my computer and placed the postcard on the scanner. I scanned the picture and enlarged it onscreen. At a greater magnification I was able to make out that the person standing behind the little girl was a man in some sort of uniform: a dark suit with big buttons on the front, and a hat. As to the thing in her hand, it looked like paper.

So all I had to do was call up everybody in Dubuque and see if they knew of a Sylvia Pershing and a little girl with a doll. That shouldn't be a problem, right? I mean, it's not like people move or die or anything.

I banged my head on my desk.

Then I heard it.

Sounded like footsteps upstairs.

I sat perfectly still and listened again. It sounded like weight against the boards, something heavy. Not like an animal. Outside, New Kassel thrived. Most of the shops had closed, but all the restaurants and the bowling alley were open. I saw people passing by the window, one girl in her swimsuit. Guess she'd just come from the lake. The sun was beginning to set, but it wasn't completely dark yet. Breaking into the Gaheimer House at such an early hour would be awfully brave for a . . . what? A burglar? A serial killer?

Maybe it was just somebody who thought the house was still open for tours. I grabbed my cell phone out of my purse and headed through the house to look.

"Hello? We're closed for tours until further notice," I called out. Nothing.

I made my way up the wide staircase, careful not to step on the stair that creaked. When I got to the top I repeated my words. Still nothing. I pushed the various bedroom doors open. There was nobody there.

I must have heard some noise from outside and thought it was inside. That made the most sense. In fact, now I wondered if this was what had happened to Sylvia that night. I'd have to ask Duran if the noise she heard was inside or outside the house.

It was an old house. Old houses make noise, that's a given.

I shook it off and went back to my office. Really, since it was daylight and people were still milling about, I thought no more of it. I logged on to the Internet and found the GenWeb page for the county of Dubuque. GenWeb is a network of genealogical pages for each state. Each page has a host and various collections of things like wills, biographies, and census records for that particular state. I e-mailed the host and told her that I had a photograph taken in 1930 and wondered if she'd take a look at it and see if she could tell me where the photograph was taken, or if she knew somebody else who could. It wasn't as much of a long shot as it might seem. If somebody e-mailed me with old photographs of New Kassel, I could most likely tell them what building was what, or at least what street the photo had been taken on. When you specialize in an area, you specialize in the area.

I shut down my computer and started to rifle through the box I had set at my feet. More receipts. I'm not sure why the woman kept every piece of paper ever given to her, but she did. Just when I was getting really bored, I found a hand-drawn picture that had been yellowed by age and obviously colored by an preschooler. In bold red outlines was the Gaheimer House. The green shutters had been colored in crookedly. A bright yellow sun with giant rays peeked out of the corner, and three people stood on the sidewalk out front. One was Sylvia, one was her sister, Wilma, and the other was a little girl.

Me.

I must have colored this for Sylvia when I was about four or five. In crooked letters I had written *To Silvera. Love Torie.*

There was no way I was going to cry. If I started to cry I might not stop, and I wasn't sure I had the energy for it, anyway. How bad is that, when you're too tired to cry?

A few hours passed, and I'd made my way through that box

started on another. This one was more recent. There were things in it from this past year. I had to pay more attention to this box, because there might be things in here that I would need. If I came across an owner's manual for the new refrigerator, though, I was going to throw it out.

What I found unsettled me all the way to my toes.

Made out to Sylvia Pershing were ten receipts for the last ten months from one Michael J. Walker, PI. *Private investigator?*

Sylvia had hired a private investigator? For what reason? And why didn't I know about it? How could I not have known about it? I searched my memory for anything unusual. Could I remember a time in the past ten months that somebody unusual had come to visit the Gaheimer House? Oh, gee, just a couple hundred tourists every week or so.

I wondered if the sheriff knew about this.

Then I wondered if Mr. Walker knew about Sylvia's death, and if he didn't, why hadn't he called here? Had he called here? Think. Think. Had a man called and hung up when I told him Sylvia was dead?

Not that I could remember. Was he still on retainer, then?

The phone rang, and I picked it up. "Torie," I said.

There was silence on the other end. "Hello?" I said. Just breathing. I slammed the phone down, irritated. I hate when people do that. Of course, now that I have caller ID in my home, it never happens. If I don't know the name or the number, I don't answer the phone. The phone-pervs can just leave a message. I didn't have caller ID at the office, though. The phone rang again, and I answered it. "Hello."

"Torie, it's Collette," a voice said. My best friend Collette, the big-city girl. Of course, the big city I refer to is St. Louis, which is pretty small in the grand scheme of cities. It's about a half hour to the north of us here in New Kassel.

"Hey, what's up?" I said. "Did you just call here?"

"No," she said.

"Oh."

"Your mom called," she said.

"My mother?" I asked. "Uh-oh."

"Yeah, she said you needed to be taken out and shown a good time."

"Oh, right. My mother did not say that!"

"Okay, not in so many words, but she said, 'Call her. She could use your contagious energy.' So I translated that to mean that I am to take you out and get you as dog-faced drunk as I can and have a great time dancing and maybe sticking some one-dollar bills in some scantily clad muscle-bound man's underwear."

"No."

"You always say no."

"I really can't. I have tons to do," I said, fingering the receipts from the private investigator.

"There's this really cool band playing in Soulard tonight," she said. "Everybody there keeps their clothes on."

"No. No offense, Collette, but I just really don't feel like it."

"Are you all right?" she asked in a slightly more serious voice. "We don't have to get wild. We could go see a movie."

"Truth is . . . I'm a bit . . . I dunno," I said, and shrugged as if she could see me.

"Depressed?"

"I am not depressed," I said. "I'm in . . . transition and it's just weird."

"You know, you deserve all that money Sylvia left you," Collette said.

"Why?"

"Because you are the only person in that town mourning her. I think she knew you would be, and that's why she left it all to you," Collette said.

"That is not true," I said. "You should have seen all the people at the funeral. The whole town showed up."

"Probably making sure she didn't jump out of the casket at the last minute," she said.

"Collette!"

"Hey, sorry, Torie, but she was a mean old bat. She was even mean to you. You just never let it bother you," Collette said.

"No," I said. "You're wrong. A lot of people loved her."

"Whatever. Last offer for a movie."

"No thanks."

"How about a pizza and conversation with your witty and wonderful best friend?"

"Sorry."

"All right, your mother can't say I didn't try," she said. "Oh, I hear Mommy Dearest is coming to town."

"I don't want to talk about it."

"You're really that upset?"

"I'm not upset because she's coming for a visit," I said. "She has the right to come for a visit. I'm upset because she's staying in my house. It's like asking a wolf to sleep in a barn with a lamb."

"You're the lamb?" she asked.

"Of course," I said.

"Just making sure."

"And I'm really upset that Rudy knows this and didn't even bother to ask me," I said. "I guess I'm really more angry about that than anything."

"Well, look at the bright side," Collette said. "By the time she leaves, your canned food will be organized by color, your plants will be organized alphabetically, your son's ears will be so clean he'll be able to hear somebody cough in Guam, and your socks will be lint-ball free."

"And I will be in an insane asylum drooling all over my nice new white suit."

Six

M y sister, Stephanie, arrived at the Gaheimer House at pre-
cisely nine o'clock the next morning.

We only met a year ago, my sister and I. She was the child of an
affair my father had. I hadn't been real keen on the idea at first.
Well, actually, I had wanted a sister all my life. It was my father's
neglect in telling me she existed that bothered me. To be even
more precise, it was the fact that he knew her, he had a relationship with her, and he had kept her from me. That was really the
thing that had hurt me. Once I got over that, Stephanie and I
bonded like . . . well, long-lost sisters.

And I forgave my father because he had finally forgiven himself.

But the great thing was, I had a sister! Somebody who was more
like me than anybody I'd ever met—except she wasn't nearly as
obnoxious as I was. Give her time.

"Good Lord, you really are pregnant," I said, smiling at her
bowling ball of a belly. Stephanie is a bit taller than I am as well as
five years younger. That hardly seems fair, I know. Being half sisters, we don't really resemble each other that much. We both have

our father's hazel eyes, but that's about it. Our similarities are more in spirit than in body.

"Yup," she said and rubbed her belly.

"But I just saw you like three weeks ago and you didn't look . . . so . . . pregnant."

"I know, the kid just suddenly grew," she said.

"How'd the doctor's visit go yesterday?"

"They're ninety-nine point nine percent sure it's a boy. Either that or it's a girl with three legs," she said.

"Cool," I said. "Matthew will have somebody to get into trouble with."

Stephanie laughed as if I were joking.

"No, you don't understand. Matthew is going to need all the help he can get against Mary."

"Oh," she said. "Right. What was I thinking?"

"Well," I said and sighed. "I need you to start by going through the boxes I've got lined up on the kitchen counter. I just want you to make piles, like utilities, private papers, legal papers, that sort of thing. Then all I have to do is look through each pile and see if there's anything I need to keep. When you're done with that, you could take all the dishes out of the kitchen cabinets."

"Why?"

"Other than a handful of things, I really don't need the dishes here. I mean, this was Sylvia's home. She lived here. I won't be living here. I just need a few things to use when I'm working."

"What are you going to do with the things you're not going to keep?"

"Well, there are things throughout the whole house I'm going to have to get rid of. Like I need twenty sets of sheets? No," I said. "I'm going to give some of it to some charities up in north St. Louis. Then I'm going to have a rummage sale or something, and with the proceeds I'm going to set up a fund of some sort in Sylvia's name."

"What sort of fund?" she asked as we began walking back toward the kitchen.

"Sylvia was Catholic," I said, "so I might set up a scholarship in her name. You know, if parents want to send their child to a Catholic school but can't afford it, the Sylvia Fund would pay for the child's tuition."

"You think you'd have enough money from one rummage sale to do that over and over?"

"Probably enough to do it a few years," I said. "And who knows? By then I'll have all our finances worked out. I could probably continue to pay it."

She nodded. "Well, I'll get started."

"I really appreciate this," I said.

"No problem," she said. "I don't get to see you enough, anyway."

I smiled. "I'll be upstairs. I'm going to start going through the bedrooms."

I couldn't help but think how morbid it was to go through a dead person's belongings. At the top of the stairs, I looked back over the balcony at the room below me. I had looked down at this view a thousand and one times, but never from the point of view of it being mine.

I was uncomfortable having to go through this woman's things, even though I'm nosy by nature. The personal and private collection of Sylvia's life was laid bare to me, and I could do with it as I chose. Rather disturbing, I thought. You can't take any of it with you, of that there is no doubt, but there was something eerie about leaving your life for somebody else to decipher, decode, dismantle, and disperse. And I wasn't even a relative.

When I reached the top of the stairs, my heart was heavy, and not from the climb. The first bedroom I came to was the first bedroom I tackled. The brown room, as I had often called it. I opened the closet door and there, hanging, ready to be worn, were Sylvia's clothes. I took them out and laid them on the bed. All of them would go to charity.

It was unbelievable what a person would find in somebody else's closets. It wasn't like I hadn't done this sort of thing before. I catalogued an estate once for Colin, but that woman, Catherine Finch, had not been my lifelong friend. It's different when you know the person. For example, I knew that the Louisville Slugger I pulled out of the closet at that moment was not, as some would suspect, for protection. No, it had come from a charity softball game we had one year, when I was only about seventeen. Sylvia had hit a home run in that game—the game-winning home run. She had been at least eighty at the time. This was the bat she had used. She had written the date with a Magic Marker on the end. It had obviously meant a lot to her. Those were things I would never have known if I'd been cataloguing the estate of a stranger.

I decided I would keep the bat for Matthew.

Farther back in the dark recesses of the closet, I found a few mousetraps—none with mice in them, thank God—and an old tripod for a camera that looked like something John Huston would have used on *African Queen*. A box of . . . shoes. A box of . . . baby shoes? They must have been hers and her sister Wilma's. They looked like miniature Mary Poppins shoes, with the hooks and the laces meandering up the ankles.

I set those on the bed. Those I would keep.

And so it went for hours. In the top of the closet I found boxes of old photographs. Now, normally this would send me into fits of excitement. Old photographs are like gold to me. In fact, I would rather relatives leave me pictures than money. Rudy laughs and jokes that if I was buried alive in a pile of old photographs, I'd die with a smile on my face. But these pictures would be frustrating for me to go through, because I knew from looking at some of Sylvia's pictures before that she probably hadn't labeled them, and the only person who could tell me who was in these photographs was now gone. So there was something else to drive me crazy. Maybe she did this on purpose.

I picked up a handful of photographs and looked at them. When I flipped them over I was stunned. Sylvia had written on the backs of most of them, and she had done it recently. The ink was new, not faded, the handwriting shakier and more unsure than a youthful hand would have been.

I flashed back to a scene of me talking to Sylvia about a year ago, when a 1920s shipwreck had been visible in the Mississippi thanks to a low water level. I had expressed my outrage over photographs she had shown me then without writing on the backs. I suppose she had realized that these photographs would go into the ranks of the unidentified, so she sat down and labeled them.

The woman would never cease to amaze me.

I took the boxes downstairs, put them on my desk, and booted up my computer. Out of the corner of my eye, I saw Stephanie go walking by but thought nothing of it. I logged on to the Internet and checked my mail. There was nothing from the Iowa GenWeb page.

Stephanie came into my office then. "How long have you been in here?"

"In my office?"

"Yeah," she said.

"About fifteen minutes," I said. "Why?"

A peculiar expression crossed her face. "I just went upstairs to ask you about this, and you weren't there, but I could have sworn I heard you up there." All I could do was stare at her. "I mean, I heard you walking. The floor creaks, you know."

"Yes, I know," I said. "I . . . well, I was here. I don't know what else to say."

"Weird," she said.

"Yeah, weird," I said. "Whatcha got?"

"Oh, should I put this in with the legal stuff?"

"What is it?"

"It looks like police reports. Or something like that. From . . . 1972."

"What?" I asked.

Stephanie shrugged and handed the papers to me. "Maybe I'm wrong on what they are. You take a look."

I took the papers from her. Indeed, they were copies of a report of some kind from the Granite County Sheriff's Department, dated October 1972. My brows creased and my head began to hurt.

"Hey, it's lunchtime," she said. "That's the other reason I was coming upstairs to get you. I don't know about you, but us pregnant ladies need to eat."

"Oh," I said. I managed to tear my eyes from the papers in my hand. She was smiling at me, a big, broad, healthy smile, although somewhere deep in the recesses of her eyes—eyes that looked just like mine, just like my father's—there was a hint of concern. "Sure. You want me to order a pizza from Chuck's?"

"Whatever. As long as it's hot and greasy."

"I think I can fulfill that request," I said and picked up the phone to call for delivery.

We ate out on the back porch, amidst the hummingbirds that dive-bombed our pizza and the wasps that went about building their nests. "I need to get somebody out here to clean up this yard. Get rid of the wasps."

"This part of the house seems more neglected," Stephanie said.

"Yeah, Sylvia wasn't much of a gardener," I said.

We ate some more, talked some more, and I was full after two pieces of mushroom and green olive pizza. Stephanie's half had mushrooms, green olives, and pineapple. She was pregnant; I'd forgive her for putting fruit on a pizza.

"Do you want me to come tomorrow?" Stephanie asked.

"Oh, you don't have to work on the weekend if you don't want."

"No, I want to help. Besides, I know the Strawberry Festival begins tomorrow."

"Ugh," I said and rested my head on the back of my chair. "I had forgotten for a while."

"Is it bad?"

"No, it's just very hectic," I said. "But it's great for the town. Except for the trampled lawns."

"Well, why don't I come and work here at the house, while you're . . . doing whatever it is you do at the festival."

"All right," I said. "My mother-in-law arrives tomorrow, too."

"Oh," Stephanie said and gave me a speculative sideways glance.

"Don't ask," I said.

Just then a man walked around the house into the backyard. He wore no shirt, his hair came down to his waist, and there were tattoos of dragons and demons all over his body. He had a ring in his nose, like a pig. "Yeah, I knocked but nobody answered."

I stood then, a bit wary. "The house is closed for tours until further notice." Maybe he couldn't read the sign, so I'd just tell him.

"I'm not here for no bloody tour," he said. "I need to set up for the gig tomorrow."

I gave Stephanie a panicked look. "Gig tomorrow? I'm sorry, there must be some mistake. We're having a Strawberry Festival. Not a . . ."

"A what?" he asked.

"Well, not something you'd most likely play for," I said.

"Really," he said and put his hands on his hips. "I like strawberries."

"I'm sure you do."

My head was spinning. Who was this guy?

"I'm with the Brown Jugs," he said.

The Brown Jugs! They were supposed to kick off the festival. I had hired them. Their Web page didn't say anything about nose rings and tattoos. The old ladies in town would keel over. My grandmother would kill me. It was supposed to be Americana and oompah music. Not . . . not . . .

"Are you Victory O'Shea?" he asked, a slight tone of exasperation in his words.

"I am," I said.

"I'm George Clarke," he said, extending a tattooed hand. "Brown Jugs."

"How do you do?"

"I'm doing great. Thanks for inquiring. So where's the stage?" He rubbed his hands together.

Seven

My alarm went off at four-thirty the next morning.

The Strawberry Festival would begin in five hours. I had to help Rudy pick up all the jars of jam, jelly, and preserves and set up all the booths. There was no point in doing any of it the night before. We had done that once several years ago. My stupid idea, by the way. In the middle of the night somebody had come with a station wagon and stolen a hundred jars of jam and preserves. My stepfather had caught them on Highway P with a flat tire and all those jars in the back of the car.

So, because of potential theft—yes, there are other idiots out there who would steal a hundred jars of jam—we wait and set up the morning of the festival. Sylvia had always been too cheap to hire a security guard to sit and watch the world famous jam overnight, but I was in charge now, and I was seriously rethinking the wisdom of such a decision, especially as I looked out the window to the pitch dark of night. There wasn't even a moon.

There was, however, a barge coming upriver. I could hear the engine through my open window. "Rudy, get up," I said, and threw a pillow at him.

My shower was quick, and it was more to wake me up than get me clean. I had barely slept. I couldn't get my mind off the things I'd found in Sylvia's house, like the sheriff's report that Stephanie had shown me. I'd read through it, and the story it told wasn't a happy one. Somebody had physically attacked Sylvia while she slept in the Gaheimer House. Of course, this had been thirty-odd years ago. I was just a small child at the time.

For a town with no secrets, this one sure seemed to have a lot of secrets. I didn't remember this event. If there was talk of it when I was a child, it had slipped through the fingers of my memory, and nobody ever mentioned it to me otherwise.

I turned off the water and grabbed my towel.

The sheriff's report had gone on to say that she had been taken to the hospital. At the bottom somebody had penciled in the date she was released, along with a list of her injuries. I suspected that was Sylvia's doing. Her injuries had included a fractured skull, fractured tibia, lacerations on her hands and arms—defense wounds, I'm certain—multiple bruises, and psychological trauma. She had not elaborated on the psychological trauma; she had only written beside it, "the desire to bury my head in the sand and never come out." Why she had requested a copy of this report and why she had kept it was beyond me.

That was what I had to lull myself to sleep with last night. In actuality, I'm not sure I ever really went to sleep. Not real sleep, where my guard is down and I rest peacefully. It was more like that kind of sleep where my mind is lost between REM and consciousness and so I never really rest.

Great. I had thousands of people to deal with today, including my mother-in-law and the Brown Jugs, and all I was armed with was deep purple circles under my eyes—and frizzy hair. We were out of conditioner.

Colin knocked on the door twenty minutes later and curled up on the couch and went to sleep. He was babysitting for Rudy and me. I can't tell you how surreal that was, to see what was once my arch-enemy curled up and drooling all over my crocheted pillows, babysitting my three children. I was going to change his name. He was going to be Grandpa with the Badge Who Drools in His Sleep.

Rudy and I drove to Virgie Burgermeister's house in silence. His desire not to speak was brought on from lack of caffeine. My desire not to speak was from anger. In fact, other than to bark an order or two, I don't think I'd spoken to him in forty-eight hours. Chuck Velasco, my husband's best friend and the owner of the best pizza place within a hundred miles, was waiting at Virgie's to help us load up the bazillion jars of jam and preserves. Virgie was awake and perky, as if she'd been up for hours awaiting our arrival. Chuck, with his muddy hiking boots and his pillow head, looked more like I felt.

When we had everything loaded, we drove down to the two-block section of town called Strawberry Center. Six booths with red and white awnings were set up in the middle of River Pointe Road, waiting to be stocked. We all unloaded the goodies, and then Rudy and Chuck left me with the job of putting all the jars into the booths while they drove Chuck's vehicle over to get the jelly from Krista.

By this point the sun was coming up over the Mississippi and bringing with it the warm temperatures of a June day in the lower Midwest. "You hungry?" I heard a voice and turned to find Helen Wickland standing there with a bag of Krispy Kreme doughnuts. The closest Krispy Kreme I knew of was up in south St. Louis County.

"Did you drive all the way up to Lindbergh for those?"

"No, the bakery in the grocery store has them now," she said, dangling the bag in front of me.

"Thanks," I said. "Just set them down. I need to get this stuff unloaded."

"I'll help," she said and set the doughnuts down. "Do you have the schedule ready for next weekend?"

"Yeah," I said. "I'll let you know which booth you're at later."

"Just making sure you're not overwhelmed," she said.

We worked side by side, Helen telling me the latest exploits of her granddaughter, who, I might add, made Mary look like a saint. By the time we had everything in order, the tourists were lined up at the entrance. The only thing that kept them from stampeding down River Pointe Road was the two deputies stationed there.

The town had come alive. Shops were open, people were in the booths, cotton candy was rotting teeth just from the smell, Kettle Korn was hot, and the funnel cakes made the whole world seem rich tasting. It was time for me to give the signal. I walked down and spoke to Deputy Miller. "Let 'em in," I said.

He nodded, and the tourists spilled into town, reminding me of a much milder version of running with the bulls in Pamplona, Spain. As long as I could keep the tourists off of the lawns of the private homes, I would consider the day a success. If I could keep George Clarke's shirt on while he sang, I'd consider it a triumph.

•

Actually, I was pleasantly surprised by the Brown Jugs. Their music was sort of like a bluegrass version of the Ramones, which was fine with me. However, the appearance of the band—and all the members were a variation on the theme of George—was quite disturbing to most of the generations who could remember the Korean War. Except my grandmother, who was seated in her usual front-row-center seat in her lawn chair keeping time with the music. She just scoffed and said, "So they look like idiots. They're just wanting attention."

I was on my way to the Gaheimer House when Eleanore Murdoch found me. Now, I love Eleanore, but I could kill her at least twice a week. She's the biggest gossipmonger in town. In fact, she writes a little column in the local paper about the goings-on of the townsfolk. She's large and top-heavy, and she wears clothes and jewelry in colors that I don't think occur naturally in the universe.

"Torie! I cannot believe you let those . . . those . . ."

"Musicians?" I said and kept walking in the direction of the house.

"Demons perform at our Strawberry Festival."

"If you don't look at them, Eleanore, their music is actually pretty good."

"Yes, but you have to look at them."

"I thought music was best appreciated when listened to with one's ears," I said.

"Torie! Torie O'Shea, you look at me right now."

I stopped walking and faced her finally. She was dressed in red-and-white gingham—I'm assuming to match the strawberry decorations—and a green hat with matching green jewelry. She really was a giant strawberry. And she was worried about the Brown Jugs' appearance? "What, Eleanore?"

"Sylvia would never have stood for this," she said.

Her words struck me hard and unexpectedly. "Well, Sylvia is not here, is she?"

"So you're just going to let our town go to hell in a handbasket?"

"Look, Eleanore, they've only got a few more songs to do and they're off the stage. But when you go back down there, I want you to look at the audience. The younger generation is really digging it. No, I would not have hired them if I had known what they looked like, and you know what? That would have been my loss. Because I think we just guaranteed that about two hundred people under the age of twenty-five will be back next year. And those young people just might learn to listen to music they might not ordinarily have tried."

To that, Eleanore had nothing to say. Her eyes bugged out of her head, and her nose instinctively angled up in the air. I expected her to cross her arms and say, "Whatever." But she didn't.

"They aren't using profanity. They're not having sex onstage. They're not even suggesting sex onstage. They're not even drinking, for crying out loud, which is more than I can say for the old farts at the bingo booth. Anything else?" I asked. "I have a lot of work to do."

She leaned in to me then and pointed a finger at me. "Don't make an enemy of me," she said.

I couldn't help it. I blurted out laughing. I was being threatened by a giant strawberry. "I would hope that the years we've known each other would count for something, Eleanore. One little band is going to make you my enemy?"

"Oh, it's one little band now," she said. "But what will it be next year? And what about the Pickin' and Grinnin' Festival? Huh? What then? Are you gonna hire that . . . Osbourne Osmond fella? Or, oh, I know . . ."

"We couldn't afford Ozzie Osbourne."

"Black Sunday!"

"That's Black Sabbath, and they don't exist anymore."

She snapped her fingers. "That serial killer guy! What's his name?"

"I don't have a clue," I said and opened the door to the Gaheimer House.

"Look, you will always be the owner of the Gaheimer House, and probably always the head of the historical society. But I can get the position of chairman of festivities taken away from you," Eleanore said. "The mayor doesn't like you, you know."

"Duh," I said. "Do what you have to, Eleanore."

I shut the door and raced to the soda machine and got a Dr Pepper. Stephanie came out of the kitchen and watched as I drank half the can without breathing.

"Bad day?" she asked.

"No, pretty average, actually," I said.

"Torie!" A voice shrieked through the living room of the Gaheimer House like a crow that had been caught in a fan. My hands began to tremble, and my eyes grew wide. Stephanie's expression owed as much to humor as it did to curiosity. "Torie O'Shea!"

"Now it's a bad day," I said.

My mother-in-law had arrived.

Eight

I plastered a smile on my face and turned to greet the senior Mrs. O'Shea. Before I had the chance to say anything, she put her hands on her hips and sneered at me. Her gray eyes narrowed, and I gulped. "Are you responsible for that band out there?" she asked.

"It's lovely to see you, Mrs. O'Shea," I said.

"Nice to see you, too, dear. Are you responsible for that band?"

"Well, yes and no. Yes, I hired them—based on a demo of their music," I said. "The Web site had no pictures of them."

"Oh, the Internet," she said and curled up her nose as if she'd smelled something putrid. "Should have known. Nothing but perverts on the Internet. Guess you learned your lesson, huh?"

"Well, uh . . ."

"Do you have a restroom?"

"Yes," I said. "Down the hall."

"Oh, is this the house that old lady left you?" She looked up at the ceiling as she headed for the restroom. "Kinda old and creepy, isn't it? But you know, Granite County has never been known for its money. All the houses down here are depressing like this."

I just shook my head as she shut the restroom door behind her. I must have stood there studying my soda can for minutes, with Stephanie watching me, but it seemed like only seconds had passed before my mother-in-law emerged from the restroom, still talking. "It also has the lowest employment rate in all of the state. It's really quite a depressed area. Why anybody would want to stay here is beyond me," she said. "Of course, I suppose there are those who get roped into living here because of elderly parents and . . . spouses that won't leave."

Do I need to translate that? I got her meaning loud and clear. "I don't think that Rudy feels trapped," I said.

The ghost of Scarlett O'Hara suddenly appeared as Mrs. O'Shea made her eyes huge and got that insipid look on her face and said, "Well, now, I never said anything about Rudolph. Don't go putting words in my mouth. I was just talking."

"Of course," I said.

"Well, now that you have all that money, you can finally get out of this place," she said. "Must be terrible knowing you can't leave a place like this. Especially when everybody around you has wanted to leave for years."

Meaning Rudy.

"I trust Rudy has taken you to the house and helped you settle in?" I said.

"He put me in this very small room. I guess it's Matthew's," she said. "By the way, Matthew looks exactly like his father. In the pictures you sent you can't really see how much he resembles Rudolph. Why, in person he's just adorable."

"This is my sister, Stephanie," I said, suddenly remembering she was standing there slack-jawed.

Mrs. O'Shea looked her up and down. "Sister? Thought you were an only child," she said.

"I . . ." I could have sworn I told her this story in the last letter I sent.

"Oh, yes," she finally said. I would have sworn on a stack of Bibles that she'd pretended not to remember I had a sister, just so the moment would be awkward and make me look bad and make my sister feel bad. Unfortunately, it wasn't exactly something I could call her on, or Scarlett O'Hara would reappear and I'd look like an idiot. "I remember now. Nice to meet you."

That was literally all she said. She turned and headed back out of the Gaheimer House, leaving Stephanie and me to stare after her. "The woman is . . ." Stephanie groped for the right words.

"Don't bother," I said.

•

"I haven't seen the woman in four years and all she can do is . . . spew hateful things!" I said. "And hateful things that aren't even true. Those statistics she uses about Granite County are twenty-five years old!"

Rudy stood in our kitchen with his arms crossed, backed up all the way against the sink. He looked sort of pasty, but there was a defiance to his expression all the same.

"Now, I want to know—and believe me, Rudolph Henry O'Shea, you'd better tell me the truth—did you tell your mother you felt trapped here in New Kassel? Tell me now. Because there's the front door, buddy. I'm not 'keeping' you here one second longer. But I'm staying."

Rudy swallowed and then gave me that expression that I could never quite pinpoint. It was part dismissal, as if I were overreacting, and part rage, because I'd hit a nerve. "Calm down."

"Explain how she got the idea that you weren't happy here," I said, trying very hard not to scream.

"She can't imagine why anybody would be happy in a small town like this—obviously she would hate it—and so therefore she assumes that I am not happy."

"Are you telling me that she just said all those things to me based on an assumption? You said *nothing* to encourage her? Because if that's the case, she is Satan. That's it, I'm calling in somebody for an exorcism."

Rudy said nothing. He just shuffled his feet.

"Rudy?" A lump gathered in my throat. Was he unhappy in New Kassel? It had never occurred to me to ask him if he was happy or not. He'd always seemed happy. He'd never mentioned wanting to move out of the area. Funny how I was ready to kick him out the door a second ago, and now I was worried he would actually go.

"All I said was that now that you had the money from Sylvia, maybe we could build a new house."

"Build a new house? Where?" I asked.

"Outside of town," he said. "But not away from New Kassel. I just meant down Highway P or something . . . or the Outer Road, where there was acreage. For your chickens. So the mayor wouldn't complain anymore. I never said anything about leaving the area."

"Well, nice of you to discuss your plans with me," I said. "Obviously you've discussed them with your mother."

"Torie, it was just said in passing. I was thinking out loud, really, not actually planning anything. It was a casual conversation we had on the way home from the airport."

"Well, if there is one thing I thought you had learned, Rudy, it is that you can't have a casual conversation with your mother. Because she takes every morsel of information and stores it up to use later," I said. "And I'm usually the target."

"I can have a conversation with my mother if I want to," he said.

"Yes, but then I have to deal with the onslaught."

He said nothing. He stewed for a minute, his gaze landing on everything from me to the kitchen floor to the clock. "You have to do something about your feelings toward my mother," he said.

"Why?"

"Because it's not healthy."

"Who are you, Deepak Chopra?"

"Because she's moving back to St. Louis."

"What?"

"This autumn."

"Oh, great. God hates me," I said. "No, no, better yet, in a former life I must have slaughtered a dozen innocent children or something, and now I'm being paid back."

"She *is* my mother. You have to deal with it."

I ignored his remark. "So are you unhappy here?" I said.

"No," he said. But his mother's poison had worked. I had already begun to believe her. And that had been her goal, after all. Just then the front door opened. It was Mrs. O'Shea coming in with my three children.

"Rudy," Mrs. O'Shea said, "whoever was that man in town stumbling all over himself and smelling like urine?"

"Bill McMullen," he answered. "Town drunk."

"And the woman with the loud mouth who looked like the giant strawberry?"

"Eleanore Murdoch," Rudy said.

"And that little skinny fella running around with pruning shears?"

"Tobias Thorley," Rudy said.

Mrs. O'Shea shook her head. "Well, I told you not to go falling in love with the mountain folk."

With that she skipped off down the hallway with my three children. I crossed my arms and glared at Rudy. "Guess I best be gettin' dat supper a-cookin,' honey. No, better yet, I be goin' out for fixin's."

Nine

I picked up Chinese food and took it back to the Gaheimer House. I booted up my computer and tried not to think of the plague that was Priscilla Louise Margaret O'Brien O'Shea. My mother-in-law liked to fancy herself full-blooded Irish, but her daughter-in-law is a genealogist, and I know better. Her grandmother's name was Schwartz.

I ate an egg roll while I checked my mail. I had an e-mail regarding the photograph of the little girl on Sylvia's postcard. It read:

> I have studied old photographs of Dubuque for close to ten years now. I can, without a doubt, tell you that your photograph is taken at the old train station. If I can be of further assistance please let me know.
> Laura James

The train station?

I heard a knock on the back door, but before I could get up and get it, someone let himself in. "It's Colin," he called out.

"I'm in my office."

"I smell Chinese food," he said as he entered the office.

Rummaging through my desk, I came up with an extra plastic fork. "Here," I said. "I'll never finish it."

"You look tired," he said. He went back and got himself a soda, then settled his butt in the chair across from my desk and began eating my Chinese food. Was it me, or did he always eat everybody else's food?

"I am tired," I said.

"What's up?"

"What, you just come by to visit? You don't visit me unless you have to," I said. "I figured that week in Minnesota was enough bonding time for you and me."

"Rudy called, said you guys had a fight," he said.

"No, we didn't have a fight. What we had was a complete refusal to see the other's opinion."

"A fight," he said.

"So what did you think, I was going to go on a crime spree or something?"

"No," he said. "It's just that since your mother is in a wheelchair and can't exactly go and see if you're all right, I sort of get delegated to do it," he said and took a bite of rice. "So, I'm here to see if you're all right, or my wife will not rest."

"Oh, you poor thing," I said. "I'm fine. There, go report to her that I was stuffing my face and happily poring over records of dead people. She'll think nothing has changed."

He didn't believe that I was all right, obviously, by the expression on his face.

"No, I'm not fine," I said, "but you can't do anything about it, and neither can my mother. However, you can do something about this." I handed him the sheriff's report from 1972. "What do you know about it?"

He scanned it quickly and swallowed his food. "How should I know anything about it? I was a sophomore in high school when this happened."

"Well, what is it all about? Sylvia was attacked? Look, you're her grand-stepnephew, don't you know anything about her?"

"I'm afraid that you knew her better than anybody," he said.

"My mom will remember this, I'm sure," I said. "I'll ask her. Might ask Elmer, too."

I thought to myself for a minute and chewed my food. "Can you find out if the guy was ever caught? If charges were ever filed?"

"Torie . . ." he began with that tone of voice.

"Look, I just want to know how the story ended," I said. "I mean, her injuries were pretty serious. An attack like that in a small town, it must have caused quite an uproar."

"I would think."

"Did you know Sylvia hired a private investigator?" I asked.

"After a scare like that," he said, "I could understand it."

"Yeah, except she hired the private investigator this past year," I said. "Not in 1972."

He stopped chewing for a moment. "Really?"

"Yes," I said. "Don't you find that odd?"

He shrugged. "Maybe."

I gave him that get-real look.

"It depends on why she hired him," he said. "If somebody skipped out on a business deal or something, I could see it."

"What if it wasn't anything like that?" I said. "What if it was for something of a more personal nature?"

"Then . . . what do you want me to say?"

"I want you to comment on her odd behavior. The alarm system, the private investigator, the two calls she made the night before she died—it appears as though she was either worried about something or afraid of something. And now I find out she was brutally attacked in 1972, right here in this house. She had a fractured skull, Colin. That's pretty damn serious."

"Maybe she was suddenly worried about a repeat of that night," Colin said.

"Okay, I can go with that, but why? After thirty-some-odd

years, why would she suddenly be worried about it?" Colin said nothing, but he was thinking what I was thinking. "Unless something happened to make her afraid," I added.

"It still doesn't mean there was anything unusual about her death."

"I'm not saying there is. I'm saying that as her friend, employee, and heir to her estate, I missed an awful lot of what was going on right under my nose."

"Maybe," he said. "Don't beat yourself up over it."

"If she was afraid and I did nothing to make her feel safe, then I am going to beat myself up over it," I said.

"You're borrowing trouble."

"Well, trouble is my middle name," I said.

"I thought obnoxious was your middle name," he said.

A cold and fake smile played at the corner of my lips. "So," I said, changing the subject from my obnoxiousness, "why do you suppose somebody would send Sylvia a postcard of a child standing at a train station?"

"Maybe Sylvia was supposed to pick her up," he said.

I sat up straight. *I think you have forgotten your promise.* Was that it? Sylvia was supposed to have picked the child up at the train station and didn't? But why the dramatics? This had happened in the thirties or late twenties. Why hadn't the person just called her up and said, "Hey, where were you?"

"Torie?" Colin said.

"What?"

"You've got that look."

"What look?"

"You know what look," he said. "And every time this happens I get a lecture from my wife on how I should have looked out for you better."

"I'm a big girl," I said. "Tell my mother that. Say, 'Jalena, she's a big girl.'"

"She's your mother," he said. "You're always going to be a child

58

to her. Don't you know once babies are born, it's your job to keep them safe? Forever. No matter how old they get."

"Bah," I said.

"I know, realistically, when they leave home you're supposed to cut the umbilical cord, but honestly, a parent never stops being a parent," he said.

"How would you know?" I said. Colin was childless.

"Because my mother told me so," Colin said. "And so has yours. Besides, you don't have to be a parent to understand that you just can't turn some things off."

There were times I underestimated him. He would never know about those times, but they did happen all the same.

Ten

The next morning I went downstairs at five o'clock to repeat the process of the morning before—only when I descended the steps I entered the land of Oz. Mrs. O'Shea had just placed a huge stack of pancakes in front of Rudy and poured him a deep and wide cup of black coffee. My kitchen sparkled and smelled of lemons and ammonia. There was not a crumb on the floor, not a speck on the counter, and the food looked scrubbed, too.

Even Fritz, my wiener dog, looked as though he'd been shampooed. Sitting under the table looking up at me with one of those purely canine expressions, he didn't seem to be too happy about it.

"Good morning, Torie," she said. "Hope you don't mind that I tidied up a bit, but I just couldn't cook with the kitchen the way it was. I realize your housecleaning day wasn't until tomorrow. Probably."

My housecleaning day was on whatever day I had the smallest amount of other things to do.

"Would you like some pancakes? I know they're Rudy's favorite."

"No, thank you," I said.

"Coffee?"

"No, thanks again." I would have day-old Krispy Kremes and warm Dr Pepper before I would eat those treacherous pancakes. She'd probably poisoned mine, anyway.

"I told the sheriff not to bother coming over this morning to watch the kids. I've got it under control," she said.

The truth was, the kids would want to spend the time with her, and that was fine, but it irritated me just a bit that she'd taken it upon herself to make that decision. It was a minor thing and from anybody else wouldn't have bothered me in the least. *Take a deep breath, Torie. It's fine. She's done nothing wrong. I'm just overreacting because she's ticked me off over everything else under the sun.*

I can't express how proud I was that I'd just talked myself out of making a big deal out of nothing. If I could just do that for the next month—several times a day—I'd survive this, and what doesn't kill you makes you stronger. I'd be in line to be the next Powerpuff Girl. I would be able to tame lions. I . . . I . . . I could bring about world peace and stop worldwide starvation.

"Oh, and really, Torie, that mayor of yours is just the most charming fella. He and I see eye to eye on a lot of issues. Especially over those chickens in your backyard. It's just a breeding ground for disease. You know, that Hong Kong flu started with chickens," she said. "The children could get the Hong Kong flu from just standing in your backyard."

The people in the world would keep on killing each other, and whoever didn't die in war would starve, and the lions would eat me, because there was no way in hell I could talk myself down from this one. So instead of putting up an argument, I grabbed the keys for Rudy's truck and headed out the door.

"Torie!" I heard Rudy call after me. "Where are you going?"

"To the freaking Strawberry Festival!" I screamed from the front porch. "Where the hell else would I be going?"

With that, I slammed the truck door, put it in gear, and headed to Virgie Burgermeister's house to gather the jams. There should be a law against demons being up and plaguing the world before dawn.

This morning went much like the day before, only it was just me and Chuck loading the jars because Rudy was still at home stuffing his face with his mama's pancakes. I said virtually nothing to anybody, and I now had a permanent crease between my eyebrows. I let the tourists in, gave them all a fake smile and fake wave, and then ran to the seclusion of the Gaheimer House, which I had decided I was never going to leave again.

My sister handed me a Dr Pepper as I came in the front door. She said nothing for several moments and then, "Do you want to talk—"

"No, I don't want to talk about it," I snapped. "Thanks for asking."

"Okay," she said. "Well, I forgot to give you this message yesterday, but there's a gentleman from the *St. Louis Post-Dispatch* who wants to interview you about your job."

"Huh?"

"He said that he'd heard wonderful things about New Kassel and all of the hard work that the historians have done to preserve the history and bring about tourism and such, and so he wants to interview you."

"Oh," I said. "That would be great for the town."

"That's what I thought," Stephanie said. "So I told him I'd call him back with a time to do the interview."

"Tomorrow is good, whenever. All we're doing here is just going through boxes and closets," I said.

"Great, I'll call right now and leave him a message."

Two hours later I was wandering around the festival, making sure everything was going as it should without too many hitches. Rachel came running up to me with one of her school friends, all smiles and giggles.

"Did you see the lead singer for that band this morning?" Rachel said. "Totally lame music, but man, was he cute!"

"You having fun?" I said

"Tons," she said.

"Where are Mary and Matthew?"

"They're with Grandma O. I think they were taking a ride on the tugboat."

"All right," I said. "Sorry I've been so busy, but you know how it's been lately."

"It's all right, Mom. Jeez, you're always there any other time," she said and shrugged. "We understand when something comes up."

I *was* always there, wasn't I? I took a moment to pat myself on the back. I went to every concert, every PTA meeting, every game, parade, open house. As I looked at Rachel, I realized that it wouldn't last forever. A few more years and she'd be looking at colleges and Matthew would be in grade school. Then it was just a few more years after that and he'd be looking at colleges and I'd be old and gray and be on my way to being Sylvia. I'm not sure how I went from patting myself on the back to depressing the hell out of myself, but I did. I think it said a lot about my state of mind at the moment.

"Oh, the pie-eating contest is getting ready to start," she said. "You gonna root for Dad?"

"I don't think so," I said.

"Oh, come on, Mom. You've rooted for him every year. Why stop now?"

We made our way through the crowd that had gathered around the table for the pie-eating contest. Rudy was wearing the same shirt he wore every year. That way, if it acquired any new stains, it wouldn't really matter. His hands were tied behind his back, but he was ready for the job. In my opinion, he had stiff competition this year. Chuck Velasco was up and smiling, Colin cracked his knuckles and then his neck before they tied his hands behind his back, and this year even the mayor had decided to give it a go. At least a dozen tourists were taking the challenge as well. There were at least a hundred pies waiting to be devoured.

In my opinion, this is a really disgusting tradition, but it was good for laughs and a great photo opportunity. "Rachel," I said, "I'm going to go get my camera."

"All right," she said.

I ran back to the Gaheimer House and grabbed my camera from

the top drawer of my desk. Then, as quickly as I could, I ran back to the contest tables. I snapped a few pictures, as did several tourists, along with Annie Boston, who often took pictures for the *New Kassel Gazette*. I moved around to get pictures from different angles, laughing all the while at the spectacle and somehow knowing that Rudy was not going to win the contest this year. Colin and Chuck actually looked hungry. Rudy was an amateur by comparison. I only hoped it wouldn't wound his pride too terribly much.

All of a sudden something or somebody hit me from behind, a blow in the middle of my back, so hard that it literally took my breath away. My camera fell to the ground. I stood there meshed in the crowd, trying to get my lungs to work. I could take air in, but nothing would go out. Nobody seemed to notice that I couldn't breathe. Everybody was busy watching the pie-eating contest. I spun around, trying to get away from all the people, where there would be more room for me to breathe, but the sun glared in my eyes. I raised my hands to shelter my eyes, and then something hit me in the stomach and knocked all the air back out of me.

Breathe in. Exhale.

It was so simple. I'd been breathing since I was born. I could do this. It was weird concentrating on something so natural.

Breathe in. Exhale.

It was only then that I realized I was being attacked. Prior to that moment I had been so concerned with just breathing that I hadn't really paid attention to the fact that this couldn't have been an accident. I saw a flash of something . . . a club, a bat . . . I couldn't be sure. A tingling spread through my chest as I put my left arm in front of my stomach to shield myself from the next blow. The crowd cheered and undulated, and when the wave of people moved, I fell to the ground, with two or three people falling backward on top of me. Luckily for me, the crowd had moved at the perfect moment, and my assailant never got to use the weapon again.

On the ground, I rolled to protect my chest as the people came crashing down on me. Somebody tripped and landed in the dirt, legs on top of mine. A huge butt smashed into my arm and then slid over to land right by my face. I covered my head as I realized that there were a dozen sets of feet within inches of me. Shouts and screams swirled around my head, and the crowd eventually parted to let in the sun. And air! Three men covered in strawberry goo suddenly appeared above me. Rudy, Colin, and Chuck.

"Holy Jesus," I heard one of them say. I wasn't sure, but I thought it was Rudy. Colin only needed one hand to pick up the people who had fallen on me. He barked some orders to the people who were within hearing distance, and they scattered like birds on the wind.

"Hang on," he said to me. "We've got a stretcher coming."

"Torie?" Rudy said. "You'll be all right, honey."

"Stay calm," Chuck said.

I have no idea why, but a vision of Moe, Larry, and Curly came into my mind as I looked up at the three of them with strawberries all down their fronts and globs of pie hanging off of eyebrows and noses.

"Somebody . . . hit me."

"I know, I know," Colin said. "Accidents like this happen at these kinds of events. Just be still. We'll get you looked at."

But there were two things I was aware of as I heard the paramedics coming with the stretcher: This was no accident. And my assailant was gone.

Eleven

I want my mother!" I barely remembered saying that over and over. After I'd spent six hours in the ER suffering various injustices to my bruised and battered body, the debate turned to where to take the now extremely drugged, swollen, and hysterical person of Torie O'Shea. I wanted my mother. Rudy wanted me to go home.

But all I could see was my mother-in-law cackling at the chance to be left alone with me. She turned into Kathy Bates in my imaginings, and I was not about to play the part of James Caan, thank you very much.

Eventually, Colin convinced Rudy that I would never calm down, so I got my way and Colin took me to their house in Wisteria.

My mother is a beautiful woman. She could easily have been a model for Raphael with that oval face and perfect skin. Polio at the age of ten had left her confined to a wheelchair for the rest of her life. It was difficult for me to grasp that she had been in a wheelchair since Bill Haley and the Comets were all the rage. But she'd managed to feed me and clothe me, and there was nobody I trusted more to tend to my wounds than my mother. Even if she didn't physically do anything, I believed that she would save me if something dreadful happened. She sat by the couch in her wheelchair, gazing down at me with that concerned look that I had come to detest. Usually that look meant that I had done something incredibly stupid, but this time I had just been minding my own business.

"You'll be happy to know that you're going to live," she said.

"Yeah," I said. "Thanks."

"You want something to drink?"

"Yes," I said. "Caffeine. Sugar. As quickly as possible."

She rolled into the kitchen. I heard her open the refrigerator and pull out a soda, then heard the tab pop. She came back in and handed the can to me. "You can't stay."

"What?" I said, taking the soda from her.

"Everybody knows Priscilla is staying with you. If you don't go home, people will talk."

"People talk anyway, like I care."

"You'll hurt her feelings," Mom said.

"In that case, I'm moving in with you," I said.

She smiled, but it didn't really reach her eyes.

"So what happened?" Colin asked as he came in the front door. "I waited until you got home to question you." He sat down in the big recliner across from me.

"Somebody attacked me."

"So you said," he began. "But how can you be sure? There were dozens of people standing around the tables."

"Somebody hit me from behind and knocked the wind out of me. When I turned around they hit my stomach. I saw the object. It wasn't just somebody bumping into me too hard."

Colin's brow creased, and he and my mother exchanged worried glances.

"This could be bad for the town, you know," he said.

"Oh, good God. We've had dead bodies in this town! How is one little accosting going to do any more damage than that?" I said.

"Well, for one thing, none of the dead bodies have ever been innocent tourists."

"I'm not a tourist."

"No, but one person over and it could have been. So the attacker picked at random and got a townsperson instead of a tourist," he said. "It could have all too easily been an out-of-towner. Plus, we've never really had anybody get hurt during a festival. A body in an abandoned building, a body at the bottom of the stairs—well, tourists don't feel threatened by those types of things. Somebody gets physically attacked at a family festival, tourists will run."

"So what do you want me to do? Lie?" I asked. "All right, Colin. The tourists decided to start slam dancing and turn the pie-eating tables into a mosh pit. It was all an accident."

"Nobody said you had to get huffy."

"For crying out loud, Colin. Look at me! I have a purple bruise on my back in the shape of South America, my stomach hurts so badly I can barely sit up, and the fat lady who sat on my shoulder gave my chiropractor enough work to keep him busy for the next two years!"

"Look, I'm not saying you shouldn't be upset. I'm just saying, why don't we take this slow and see if anybody else saw anything before we start coming out and saying you were mugged."

"Fine, whatever. Did anybody find my camera?"

"Rachel did," he said. "She's pretty shook up."

"Poor kid. So I really can't stay here?" I asked and tried my best to look pitiful.

"You can stay a day or two," Mom said. "Anything more than that and it will look like you're avoiding your mother-in-law."

"I *am* avoiding my mother-in-law," I said. "But it's more than that. It's self-preservation."

My mother *tsked* me as mothers do.

"Fine, I'll go home tomorrow," I said. "Can I just lie here on the couch and wallow in misery for one night? Just one night? Huh?"

"Sure, go ahead," Colin said.

He and my mother both headed out of the living room, and I grabbed for the television remote. I never had control of the remote at home. "I know what I saw," I said to Colin as he left.

That night, for the first time in weeks, I slept really well. That was the painkillers at work. I didn't care what it was; the fact was, I had gotten my first good night's sleep in a long time, and that was all that mattered. At about nine o'clock in the morning somebody knocked on my mother's front door. Colin had gone to work, and my mother was in the bathroom, so I shuffled to the front door, ooching and ouching all the way.

The man at the door extended his hand. "Paul Rossini," he said. *"Post-Dispatch."*

"Not today," I said. "I'll reschedule. Have a good day." I shut the door and headed back to the couch.

He resumed knocking, and I threw the pillow across the room. Like that was going to help. He just kept knocking and asking to speak to Torie O'Shea. I tried to imagine that he was a woodpecker, but it wasn't working. Finally I went to the door again, cussing all the way.

"Forgive me, but I really can't do this today," I said as I opened the door. "How did you know where I was, anyway?"

"Your sister said you were under the weather and staying with your mother. It wasn't hard to find out who your mother was."

"Look, I had a really bad day yesterday," I said, "and I don't much feel like talking. In fact, I wouldn't talk to God right now if he knocked on the front door. It hurts to breathe, it hurts not to breathe. My head hurts. And my medication is making everybody sound like they're in a tin can. I really need to reschedule."

"But I need to do this interview today if you want the article to run before next weekend."

"Well, then I'll just pass."

"You're right," he said. "An article about crime in a small midwestern town would probably go over much better than an article about peace and prosperity."

"You . . ." I sputtered. "Fine, come in. But you're going to have to use a stock photo. I'll give you one."

He held his hands up. "I just want the story."

"Have a seat," I said, and struggled to sit down with as little pain as possible.

"So tell me your background."

"You don't have time for my background, but suffice it to say I grew up here, went to school here, married here, and settled here. My parents weren't natives, though. They moved here when I was born."

"How long did you know the Pershing sisters?"

"All of my life."

"What made you decide to go to work for them?"

"Well, my major was history, and I'm a genealogist. Sylvia offered me a job with flexible hours, a job where I could do what I loved. She was also a friend of my mother's. I took it."

"How do you account for the success of this town?" he asked. "I mean, it's in a depressed area."

"It is not a depressed area," I said, thinking that the next person who said the word "depression" or any variation of it would find his teeth in his stomach. Or hers.

"Recently Granite County has been coming into its own," he said, "but even five years ago it was mostly farms and trailer parks."

"What are you insinuating?" I said.

"Nothing," he said. "It's just that somehow, in the middle of all of this, there is this town, New Kassel. A little gem. A tourist attraction. And it's been making money since 1990. There's never a weekend that is not packed with people. The true sign of success is the fact that there are tourists here during the week as well. How do you account for that?" he said.

"Well, first of all, New Kassel is not the only decent place in Granite County. Wisteria is a very fine city," I said.

"Yes, of course," he answered. "But people don't say, 'I'm going to Wisteria this weekend.' They say, 'I'm going to New Kassel.' Why do you think that is?" he asked.

"Two words," I said. "Sylvia Pershing."

He wrote something down on his pad of paper and then looked at me for more.

"Sylvia loved New Kassel. And she loved it for lots of reasons.

Part of it was, she knew how important the town had been in the nineteenth century. It was a major stopping point along the Mississippi, especially between Memphis and Minnesota. I think she remembered the New Kassel of her youth as a magical place, and she wanted to keep that going. But it was her shrewd sense of business that made her realize that there was money to be made here," I said. "You see, in the seventies especially, around the Bicentennial, a new interest in our past came alive. Prior to that you had the whole thing going on in the sixties that said everything that was old was bad. But the Bicentennial really raised an awareness of who we were and what we were born of. A newfound interest in antiques emerged. Things like quilting, which had been looked at as something old ladies did on Sundays, suddenly took on a new meaning. People under forty started quilting. Sylvia saw that and cashed in on it."

"How exactly do you think she 'cashed in' on it?" he said.

"Well," I said. I hadn't even brushed my teeth yet, and I found the physical act of talking very taxing. Yes, Torie O'Shea was tired of talking. There was also an aching in my joints that was telling me it was time for my medicine. Still, this was my chance to tell Sylvia's story, so I took a deep breath and did what I do best: talk. "It began with her buying real estate. She realized that the only way to get the town to be presentable for tourists was to give all the buildings face-lifts. I mean, there were homes where people had derelict cars in the front yard, and mud ponds for lawns, and paint peeling off of the clapboards. Not all of the houses were like that, but too many for the town to ever go over as a center for tourism. Now, she couldn't exactly go up to these home owners and say, 'Clean up your yard.' Those were their houses, and they could do what they wanted. So she began buying buildings along River Pointe Road and then selling them as commercial. If they were businesses, they'd be kept up."

"Ah," he said as he wrote furiously.

"Then she began buying homes, and instead of selling those, she rented them. That way, she *could* say, 'Clean up your yard,' and they'd have to do it. Pretty soon the main part of town was either Sylvia's or had been Sylvia's, and everything was presentable."

He looked at me expectantly.

"That's it, really. I mean, she invested everything she had and made money and made the town what it is today. She then began the historical projects, which were accumulating and preserving the history of all the buildings in town, and then all the families. We began cataloguing the cemeteries. So when you come to New Kassel, it's not just for the fudge, or the pastries at Pierre's, or even the music. You come because it's an old town that's been preserved, a place where you can stay at the Murdoch Inn, look out on the river, and get a glimpse of life in another time."

"I see," he said. "Back when things were slower."

"Simpler," I said.

"Are the hotels and bed-and-breakfasts often full?"

"There are no hotels. You'd have to come here to Wisteria for a hotel. But there are several B-and-B's, and yes, they are often full, especially when we have festivals and the like. I think people also come from out of town to visit St. Louis, and they stay down here and just commute to all the activities. It's not that much of a drive."

He made some more notes, and I was beginning to wonder if he was ever going to leave.

"Now, what is your part in all of this?" he asked.

"My part?"

"Yes. You inherited the title of president of the historical society, correct?"

"Well, no, not exactly. It's not a title that can be inherited. Things are in disarray right now, with Sylvia just having passed away. Soon, we'll gather the members of the historical society and have a vote on it. I do own the Gaheimer House, which is where the historical society is housed."

"So you own the Gaheimer House. Which is what? The main focus of the town, right? I mean, that is the house Ms. Pershing inherited from one of the wealthier townspeople, correct?"

"Yes," I said and wondered where he'd gotten his information.

Clearly he'd either done some bang-up research or spoken to somebody in town who knew a lot and talked a lot.

Eleanore Murdoch.

"So why did she leave it to you?" he asked.

"I'm not sure," I said, "other than because I was a friend of hers. I'd worked alongside her for years. We had the same vision."

"That's quite a bit to leave to a friend. I mean, did she leave you everything?"

"That's really not the point of this interview," I said, "but Sylvia had nobody else to leave it to. She had no children. She'd outlived everybody, even her own nieces and nephews. She had a few great-nieces and -nephews, but none of them had much to do with her or cared about her."

"How convenient for you," he said.

I suddenly arrived at the conclusion that I didn't like him very much.

"So Wilma Pershing left everything to Sylvia and Sylvia left everything to Wilma in their original wills, with the agreement that whoever died last would leave everything to you."

Chills danced down my spine. "How do you know that?" I asked.

"I'm a journalist."

"All right, Mr. Rossini, let me rephrase that. Why is it so important for you to know what the terms of their wills were?" I said.

"Has anybody contested the will?"

"No."

"You're the executor and beneficiary?"

"This interview is over. This has nothing to do with New Kassel."

I stood to show him to the door.

"I think it has a lot to do with New Kassel. The people of New Kassel might like to know how this all came about. I mean, since now you own half of their town."

I whirled on him. "The people of New Kassel do know how it all came about," I said. "There's no secret here."

"Were you upset that it took the Pershing sisters as long to die as it did?" he asked.

"Why, you . . ." I grappled for the words. "I had no idea I was being left anything. And I think you'd better be leaving before I call my stepfather home from work. He's the sheriff, you know."

Mr. Rossini held his hands up in surrender. "Just trying to find out how a college dropout manages to put herself in a very lucrative situation."

"I didn't put myself anywhere, Mr. Rossini, but I'm going to put my foot somewhere if you don't get out of this house, now."

He smiled, and the faintest touch of pink shaded his ears. With no further ado, he left my mother's house, and I hobbled to the kitchen to find my pain pills. I'd better take two.

At that point my mother wheeled in, and I put the extra pill back in the bottle. Funny how the very presence of your mother can make you do the right thing.

"Who was that?"

"Journalist."

"Oh."

"Works at the same paper as Collette, so I may have some words with her," I said.

"Interview didn't go well?" she asked.

"Not really," I said. "Look, I'm going home now. I need a shower, and I need to brush my damn teeth."

THE NEW KASSEL GAZETTE
The News You Might Miss
by Eleanore Murdoch

Tragedy has hit the Strawberry Festival!

What is our town coming to when one of its best known citizens is struck down, right there on the street, with a vile and evil instrument of terror! Everybody lock your doors. Bring your dogs in at night. I haven't seen this level of terror in the folks of New Kassel since the body was discovered on the banks of the Mississippi! Where are our brave law enforcement officers?

Tobias said to tell whoever dumped the horse manure in his backyard, thank you.

The winner of the Pierre's Bakery raffle was none other than Jalena Brooke. I don't think that's quite fair since she no longer lives in New Kassel. She moved to Wisteria to be with her new husband. But, regardless, she has won a month's supply of bagels!

Until next time,

Eleanore

Twelve

I wasted the entire day lying in my bed, staring at the ceiling. I stared at the ceiling for a solid six hours. Sometimes it was fuzzier than other times, and sometimes I drifted off to sleep, but always I woke up and resumed my state of stupor watching a ceiling that was never going to change. At least not quickly enough for me to see.

Rudy had left a note saying his mother had Matthew for the day, and I was actually grateful for that in my present state. By the time the girls came in from school around three, it was a good thing, because I think I was actually beginning to warp the ceiling with my gaze.

"Mom?" Rachel asked as she came up the stairs.

"Yeah?"

"Are you all right?"

"I'm fine." Mothers lie. Don't ever think they don't.

"Does it hurt?" She sat on the edge of my bed. There was real concern in those deep dark brown eyes.

"Yes."

"Man, that was freaky. Like, one minute you were there taking pictures and the next minute you were on the ground being trampled."

"You see anything?" I asked.

"No, Dad barfed and I was busy watching him."

"Oh."

"I got an A on my science test today."

"Way cool," I said. "Hey, you guys wanna go get some pizza?"

"Shouldn't we wait for Dad and Grandma O?"

"Yes," I said. "I meant when they got home. I don't feel much like cooking."

"Grandma would probably cook for you."

"She's going to be here awhile," I said. "May as well not burn her out in the first week."

"Okay," she said.

"Where's Mary?"

"Downstairs," Rachel said. "She's got a black eye."

A black eye. Just so casual. You had to love teenagers. They could be absolutely manic over the most minor things and so nonchalant over serious matters. "And she got this how?"

"She walked under the monkey bars and somebody kicked her in the face."

"Oh," I said. "Well, at least it wasn't anything deliberate. I figured she'd be up here showing it off."

"Somebody told her to put meat on it, and so she's downstairs opening the bologna," Rachel said.

"Great."

•

Velasco's Pizza is probably one of my favorite places in the world, with its 1950s decor and red vinyl seats and the best pizza in three different styles: Chicago, New York, and St. Louis. And the owner, Chuck Velasco—Rudy's best friend—is one of my favorite people. My mother-in-law had lifted her nose to an angle I didn't think was humanly possible when I had announced we were going out for pizza, and she didn't lower that nose once we got to Velasco's. In fact, Mrs. O'Shea wiped the seat with her hanky before she sat down, managing to keep that nose in the air the whole time.

"Hey, loser," Chuck said and slapped Rudy on the back.

"Hey, I would have won if I hadn't eaten all those pancakes for breakfast," Rudy said.

"Cry me a river," Chuck said. "What's it gonna be tonight?"

We ordered our pizza, Mrs. O'Shea ordered a salad and a beer, and we fell into a nice familial conversation about the dangers of walking under the monkey bars on a playground and how it was similar to walking behind somebody on a swing. Mary was actually quite proud of her badge of courage, as if she had gone through some rite of passage. Our conversation didn't last long, though, since I was approached by three different people who wanted to talk to me. One person paid me his rent, so that was fairly easy, except it seemed to me that everybody in the parlor stopped and stared as the check changed hands. One person asked if we could get the roof fixed in the house she was living in—since we now owned it—and another wanted to know if I could give her a job.

When our food arrived, Mrs. O'Shea bowed her head, made the sign of the cross and, stared at us. The five of us looked at each other, and Rudy made the sign of the cross and, as the girls giggled, proceeded to say grace. There would be talk in the gossip column tomorrow that the O'Shea family had said grace in public.

"So, Torie, I realize you're not Catholic," Mrs. O'Shea said, "but you shouldn't keep your husband and children from going to church."

There are times when I should be given an award for not acting on every impulse that comes into my head. If I did, her lips would now be sewn shut with baling wire, and the fact that they were still free to flap about and insult me was a shining example of what a great person I was.

"Mom," Rudy began.

"Don't 'Mom' me," Mrs. O'Shea said. "You haven't been to church since you got married."

"This has nothing to do with me," I said. "Rudy can get up and go to church any time he wants."

Mrs. O'Shea rolled her eyes and waved a hand at me.

"Rudy," I said, turning to him, "do I keep you from going to church?"

"No," he said. "In fact, you've encouraged me, and I just don't ever seem to go."

"There," I said and looked back to Mrs. O'Shea.

She just ate her salad in silence with tiny bites, ever so ladylike. I stared at her the whole time she ate, waiting for her to acknowledge what Rudy had said. She never did. Instead, she downed her beer in three large swigs, the complete opposite of the way she had eaten the salad. "Did you hear him?" I asked.

"Torie," Rudy said and laid a hand on my arm.

"The fact is, Torie," she said, "my son was a perfectly good Catholic boy until he met you. So there's the evidence."

I should have probably just shut up and thought about cute fat puppies, but I couldn't. "I would like to know one thing," I said.

Rudy covered his eyes and shook his head. Mary smiled and came to attention.

"Why is it that I get blamed for anything Rudy does that you don't approve of? It never once occurred to you that maybe this is the real Rudy O'Shea, and now that he's a free man, out of the chokehold of his mother, he can be who he really is. I don't hold a knife to his throat over anything, Mrs. O'Shea. Never have."

At that moment I felt like I was trapped in some horrible *Monday Night Movie*, as Mrs. O'Shea leveled a gaze on me that would have ripped me apart if I hadn't been prepared for it. The venom was palpable, and the air seemed to grow ten degrees hotter in ten seconds flat. Even Matthew had grown still.

"Torie," Rudy said again.

"What?" I said. "Why is it so hard for you to just tell her the way you feel about things? I do. It's really easy. Here, let me show you—"

"You may leave this table at any time," Mrs. O'Shea said in a cold and steely voice.

"Excuse me?" I said.

"I'll not tolerate—"

"You don't have the right to tolerate or not tolerate. Who do you think you are?" I said.

"Mom," Rachel said.

"What?"

"People are staring."

Sure enough, I had been yelling and didn't even realize it. The entire restaurant was staring at our table. I had managed to make myself look like an ass, even when I was right. You know, when I think about it, that's what Mrs. O'Shea did best. She always made me look bad when she was in the wrong. That was a true artist.

I went about cutting up my pizza with such fury that I knew there were knife marks left on the plate. I ate in silence—chewing my food as if I had an outboard motor attached to my jaws—and looked at no one.

"I have a volleyball game tomorrow," Rachel said.

"I know," I said. "I'll be there."

More silence.

Just then my sister burst through the front door of the pizza parlor. She glanced around the room, and when she found me she ran over to the table. "Oh, thank heavens you're here," she said.

How do people always know where I am?

"What?" I said. "Are you all right? Is the baby okay?"

"No," she said. "And yes."

"What, then?"

"You need to come over to the Gaheimer House right away."

Thirteen

The Gaheimer House is haunted," Stephanie said, breathless, as we jogged along the sidewalk of River Pointe Road.

"Steph, stop running, you're going to hurt the baby," I said. Not to mention my whole body still ached from yesterday. In fact, I think it hurt worse than yesterday, and I could barely keep up with her.

"Please, Torie," she said. "I'm fine. I walk four miles every day."

"You do?" I asked. "On purpose?"

"Yes," she said. "You walk more than that."

"True," I said. Unless I had the kids with me or I was bringing home groceries, I usually walked everywhere I went. The benefits of living in a small, self-contained town. "Wait, did you say the house was haunted?"

"Yes," she said as we arrived in front of the Gaheimer House.

"You dragged me out of dinner with my . . . my mother-in-law to tell me the Gaheimer House was haunted?"

"Yes."

"Oh, I love you!" I said and flung my arms around her. "You are so ingenious. I would have never thought of it."

"Torie," she said, "I'm dead serious. In fact, I am so dead serious that I am not going back in the house alone ever again."

I stared at her long and hard. She wasn't flighty, nor was she the type to be rash or jump to conclusions, and I saw no traces of humor on her face. I looked at the house, and chills danced down my spine. I didn't think for one minute that the house was haunted. What I did think was that Stephanie had heard something while she was alone in the house. Just like I had. Just like Sylvia had.

"Did you call the sheriff?"

"Not for a ghost, and the last time I checked Spooky Fox Mulder had hung up his supernatural phenomena badge, so that leaves you," she said.

"Steph, there are no such things as ghosts," I said.

"I know that," she said, "but you might want to tell that to the ghost in that house."

I took my cell phone out of my purse, dialed the sheriff's station, and got Deputy Duran. "This is Torie O'Shea."

"Oh, hi, Mrs. O'Shea."

Mrs. O'Shea? Nobody calls me Mrs. O'Shea. Everybody in this town has known me forever and a day. "Uh . . . yeah, listen, we've got a problem at the Gaheimer House," I said. "I think there's an intruder or a prowler or something. Can you send somebody to check it out?"

"Newsome is a few blocks over. I'll send him."

"All right," I said and hung up. "Newsome's coming. We stay outside until he gets here."

"You don't have to convince me," she said and crossed her arms.

While we were waiting, the buildings on the opposite side of the street began to glow with the orange of the setting sun, and I couldn't help but think how brave this prowler was. This was two or three times now that somebody had heard something in the Gaheimer House in broad daylight.

Mayor Castlereagh pulled up then but didn't turn off his engine—which was good, because that meant I only had to tolerate him for a few minutes. "Whatsa matter, Torie? You get locked out of your new mansion?" he asked from the window of his car. He was a short, pudgy man with a shiny head and a burning hatred for little old me.

"No," I said. "Thanks for your concern."

"Hear you're moving," he said. "Finally get rid of those damn chickens."

"You're moving?" Stephanie asked me.

"No, I'm not moving," I said. "In fact, if I were, I wouldn't now just because he wants me to."

"I told you," he said. "I told you I'd get rid of those chickens one way or another. You know, your mother-in-law agrees with me."

"Oh, well, then that settles it, doesn't it?" I said. "When two great minds get together and pass judgment on a bunch of chickens, they must be right."

"Don't push me, Torie."

"You know, your term's gonna end soon," I said.

"What's that supposed to mean?"

"That means you won't be mayor forever."

"Are you threatening me?"

"No, I'm telling you that maybe somebody worthy will run against you next year and you can finally retire and bowl all day. Oops, you do that *now*," I said and covered my mouth.

He was about to say something more when Deputy Newsome pulled up in his patrol car and stepped out. The mayor drove away, and Stephanie looked at me as if seeing a new person. "Sorry, I'm in a really bad mood," I said.

"Does everybody hate you?" she asked.

"No, just the mayor and my mother-in-law. Well, and maybe Eleanore, but only sometimes. No, actually, now that I think about it, I think it's just the mayor and my mother-in-law," I said.

"And your stepfather," she said.

"No, Colin doesn't hate me. He hates some of the things that I do. There's a difference," I said. "Which I've learned in the past few years."

"Ahh," she said as if she totally understood. Maybe she did.

"Oh, and by the way, don't ever tell a reporter where I am," I said.

"Oh, it didn't go well?"

"No. The guy was a total jerk."

"I'll remember that," she said.

Deputy Newsome walked up next to us on the sidewalk. "What's the problem?" he said.

"I think the house is haunted," Stephanie said.

"Well, I ain't no Ghostbuster," he said and laughed at his own joke.

"I think she heard a prowler," I said.

"That I can check out," he said. "You ladies stay out here."

"I heard it upstairs!" Stephanie called out after him. That's exactly where I had heard it, too. In Sylvia's room.

Stephanie and I talked a few minutes about some of the things she had found during my day of lying in bed and staring at the ceiling. After about ten minutes, Deputy Newsome stepped out and onto the sidewalk. "I didn't find anything," he said.

"How can that be?" Stephanie asked.

"He or she could have easily left while you ran to get me," I said.

"What's more, I see no evidence that anybody was even in the house," Newsome said. "I mean, nothing was out of place upstairs at all. Not like anybody was looking for anything."

"This makes no sense," Stephanie said. "This isn't the first time I've heard something."

"Look, I heard something upstairs the other day, too. And Sylvia, well, we know Sylvia heard something the night before she died," I said. "What can we do about this?"

Newsome shrugged.

"Have you noticed anything missing?" Deputy Newsome asked.

"No," Stephanie said. Looking to me she raised her eyebrows. "Have you? You'd know better than I."

I thought for a moment. I had given some things away already, and the place was certainly in disarray what with all the boxes and everything. "Maybe a few things, but nothing of any value."

"Like what?" he asked.

"I don't know. I'm not even sure now that I've said it. I mean, look at the place," I said.

He glanced around and wrote something down on his notepad.

"Um . . . a ring," I said. "It was my favorite of her rings and I haven't seen it in awhile. But really, it's not worth anything. So, it's probably here somewhere."

Newsome wrote a few words again. Finally, I waved my hand in the air. "No, now that I think of it, I really don't think anything is missing. I'm sure it's here somewhere."

"You need to make sure you're locking the doors once you're inside and set the alarm. I know it's a pain in the butt to mess with the alarm every time you go in and out, but you're just going to have to remember to set it when you're inside. That's all I can tell you," he said. "Or maybe I can get the sheriff to post a watch for a couple of days. We're not busy. Not until the weekend for the second half of the festival."

"All right," I said. I worked my lower lip between my teeth, wondering, although what I was wondering wasn't quite fully formed yet. It was just this vague ghost of an image swimming around in my head. Whatever it was, it made me uncomfortable.

"At any rate, I don't think he'll be back tonight," Newsome said.

"I'm not going back in there," Stephanie said. "Not tonight."

"That's fine," I said. I reached out and squeezed her hand. "You go on home."

"I'll be back tomorrow. Will you be here?" she said.

"Yeah, I'll be here," I said.

"I'll walk her to her car," Newsome said to me, which I was relieved to hear.

The two left me standing on the sidewalk trying to decide what to do next. I looked up at the redbrick building and thought, *I can't let it scare me.* The Gaheimer House was mine now, and I had to make sure that it was treated with respect and taken care of, just as

Sylvia had, or all of Sylvia's hard work and dreams would come crashing down. There was no such thing as a ghost, and Newsome had said the prowler—if there had been one—was gone. I placed my hand on the doorknob and opened the door. When I stepped up the high front step my back seized, and I took a deep breath to try to quell the pain.

Then it hit me. The incoherent mix of thoughts I'd had earlier suddenly jelled. What if the person who attacked me at the Strawberry Festival had picked me on purpose? What if it hadn't been a random assault? What if it had been the same person who kept appearing and making ghost noises in Sylvia's bedroom? And what if Sylvia's attack in 1972 was somehow connected? I was probably reaching on that last one.

I looked back over my shoulder as the river slipped into the dark purple glove of dusk. Was the attacker watching right now? Was he hiding across the street behind the shops?

I shut the door and set the alarm.

Then I made my way to my office, looking over my shoulder the whole way. I rifled through my desk until I found the name of the private investigator Sylvia had hired. Michael J. Walker. I picked up the phone and dialed the number. I got a recording. I left my name and all my phone numbers and told him to call me right away, that it was urgent.

Then I decided that I wouldn't get any work done in this house this evening, so I grabbed a few boxes of things and headed out. By the time I made it to the front door, I had to stop to catch my breath. It felt like somebody had pulled all my tendons out of my joints, and all I had done was carry a few boxes a few dozen feet. My cell phone rang just as I picked up the boxes again. I set the boxes down and answered it. It was Rudy.

"Is everything all right? Was there a break-in?" he asked.

"Not sure," I said. "We think somebody's been in the house, but everything seems to be in order. Are you still at Velasco's?"

"Yeah," he said.

"Can you come by and give me a ride home? I've got some boxes of pictures I want to work on, and I don't want to carry them all the way home."

"Sure," he said. "I'll be right there."

Fourteen

A t home, I read Matthew a bedtime story—one with dinosaurs, of course—and helped Mary with her math homework, which was sort of like the blind leading the blind. Rachel flung history questions at me the whole time I was helping Mary with her math. "What prince of England died on board the *White Ship* in 1120?"

"Oh, um . . ." I snapped my fingers. "William. Son of Henry the First."

"Oh, you answered my second question, too," she said. "And who did Henry the First kill—it is rumored—to get the crown of England?" Rachel read aloud from her history book.

"His brother. Also a William. You know, these answers are probably in your book," I said.

"He killed his own brother and got to become king?" she asked, ignoring me. "So, like, I could kill Mary and become president?"

"No," I said. "And they can't prove that he killed his brother. It's just awfully mysterious that his brother was hunting and was shot by a stray arrow and Henry just happened to be hunting in the same forest at the same time and oops! Now Henry is king of England.

But, you know, Henry lost his only male heir later when the *White Ship* went down, so you have to wonder."

"Wonder what?" she asked.

"Well, all bad deeds eventually get punished, in some form or other. If King Henry did kill his brother to steal the crown of England, then you have to wonder if Henry sort of got his payback when his son went down with the *White Ship*. If he had never become king, his son would probably have never been in that position. So you could say he set his own son's fate by taking what wasn't his to take."

Rachel stared at me. "Mom, your mind is wicked."

"Sorry," I said.

"No, Mom," Rachel said and wrote furiously. "I mean you're brilliant."

"Oh," I said. "Wicked as in good. I gotcha."

"Of course, that's just one way of looking at it. But you know what they say: Whatever we do comes back to us twofold."

"Mom," said Mary, "just who is 'they' when people say 'you know what they say'?"

"I'm not sure," I said and scratched my head.

"Mom," Mary said, "what is eight times seven?"

I counted on my fingers. "Fifty-four."

"Fifty-six!" Rachel said.

"Oh, sorry," I said.

"Okay, so who inherited the title from Henry the First, and how did this affect England?" Rachel asked.

"Well, his daughter, Matilda, actually inherited the title, but not for very long. The king's nephew Stephen—who was also supposed to sail on the *White Ship* but got off at the last minute—made a claim on the throne, and this was bad for England because total anarchy ensued. Most of the nobility weren't ready to follow a woman, but some were, so you had this big disagreement and so forth."

"You know all of that without even looking at my book?" she said.

"History is my thing," I said and shrugged. It's totally useless in the everyday world, by the way.

"Mom," Mary asked, "what is forty-three divided by four?"

"Uh . . . where's that calculator?"

"What nationality by blood was King Henry the First?"

"French."

"So the king of England was French?"

"Yeah," I said. "Long story. Later the kings of England would be German."

Rachel rolled her eyes.

"Mom, what is forty-three divided by four?"

"I'm working on it," I said, punching numbers on the calculator. "Oh, you figure it out. It's your homework."

When homework was finished, I retired to my bedroom upstairs while Rudy and his mother watched some sitcom reruns. I had to laugh, because she had refused to let the television land on ESPN since she'd been here. Maybe Rudy was having to suffer after all.

Safe in my blue-gingham bedroom, I tore into the boxes that I'd brought from the Gaheimer House. I tried to make piles as I went through the photographs. One pile was for photographs of places: buildings, businesses, etc. Those could be used in the future for special displays and even publications with historical content. I found an excellent photograph of the Murdoch Inn back before it was the Murdoch Inn, when it was owned by the Queen family. In another pile I put photographs of people I knew, like Sylvia and Wilma, or even people who had died before I was ever born, if I knew of them or knew their families. Another pile was for people about whom I didn't have a clue.

I was extremely excited by the pile of "places" pictures. There were some absolute gems in that pile. In fact, I was getting ideas for their use with every photograph I picked up. It was the pile of "unknowns" that interested me the most, though. All the pictures had been written on, but I still didn't know who they were. I believed one was Sylvia's mother, since she looked just like Sylvia had when she was a young woman and it was taken around the 1890s, but I'd have to check Sylvia's family tree to match up the name. Some people in the pictures had the last name Pershing, so obviously they were Sylvia's paternal relatives.

My heart stopped as I came to a photograph of a little girl. I rummaged through my drawers for my magnifying glass. I found it, placed the picture as close to my desk lamp as possible, and looked at it under the magnifier.

It was the same little girl whose face had been haunting me for the past few weeks.

I flipped the photograph over with my eyes shut, hoping there would be a name on the back of it. When I opened my eyes, sure enough, written in somebody's loopy penmanship were the words *Millie O'Shaughnessy.*

There was no year given, but she looked to be about a year younger than she was in the train-station postcard photograph. That would make it 1920s or early '30s.

"So, little Millie O'Shaughnessy. Who *are* you?"

Just then my phone rang. The caller ID read WALKER, MICHAEL J.

Fifteen

Hello?"

"May I speak to Torie O'Shea?" the voice said.

"This is she," I said.

"This is Mike Walker. You left a message for me."

"Mr. Walker, I'd like to hire your services," I said.

"I charge twenty dollars an hour, plus expenses," he said.

"Fine." Boy, he didn't mess around. He got right down to business.

"Can I meet with you?" he asked.

"Sure," I said.

"When is convenient for you?"

I looked at the clock on my desk. Eight-forty. "If you're not too far from me I can meet you this evening," I said.

"This isn't a cheating husband case, is it?" he asked.

"No."

"Because those suck. I always get depressed when I do those."

"No, it's not a cheating husband case," I said.

"All right," he said. "I live in Crestwood. Know where that is?"

"Yes," I said. "It'll take me forty-five minutes to get there."

"Well, then, how about we meet somewhere central?" he said. "You pick."

"Meet me at Frailey's Bar and Grill on Butler Hill in South County," I said.

"That right there at 55, by the Schnucks?"

"Yes," I said.

"All right," he said. "I'll be there in about twenty minutes."

I put on a pair of good jeans instead of the holey ones I had been wearing, pulled my hair up in a ponytail, grabbed my purse, and ran down the stairs. Rudy and his mother were both snoring in front of the television, which they both would deny later.

I tapped Rudy on the shoulder, and he jerked awake. "What? Where are you going?"

"I've got my phone with me," I said. "I'm going up to Frailey's in South County."

"Why?"

"I'm going to meet . . . a client."

"A what?" He rubbed his eyes.

"I'll be back in about an hour," I said and headed for the door.

"Who the hell wants their family tree traced at this hour?" he asked.

I just smiled and shut the door.

I drove up Highway 55 with the radio on, wondering exactly what it was I would say to Mr. Walker. I hadn't expected him to call tonight, so I hadn't rehearsed my speech. After about ten minutes on the road, I passed the exits for Imperial, Richardson Road, and Highway 141 in Arnold—with that ugly green water tower—then got into the right-hand lane, because my exit was coming up. Meramec Bottom Road passed, and I put my blinker on as the sign for Butler Hill came up over the road. I made a left and crossed back under the highway to the plaza with the giant Schnucks supermarket and Frailey's Bar and Grill. I had made it in twenty-five minutes. I jogged up to the front door.

Having eaten here, I can tell you it is the food that sets Frailey's apart from the other sports bars, not the décor. The inside of Frailey's is like every other sports bar in the Midwest. Sports paraphernalia hung from the walls. What looked like ten televisions hung from the ceiling, all with different sports events on. Poor Rudy. Stuck at home watching sitcoms. The hostess greeted me, and I told her I was meeting somebody.

"Will you need a table?" she asked. That translated into "We're getting ready to close the kitchen."

"No, we'll sit at the bar," I said.

Her face brightened a bit at that. I didn't blame her; who wanted to be stuck at work because of one customer who came in ten minutes before the kitchen closed and then took two hours to eat?

"I'm just going to stand here and wait for someone," I said.

"Sure," she said.

Within two minutes a man walked in. He looked to be about thirty and was wearing a Rams sweatshirt, jeans, and cowboy boots. "Hey!" he said. "Are you Torie? I'm Mike Walker." He stuck his hand out for me to shake, which I did. He seemed very . . . young. A worn and disgusting toothpick hung out of his mouth as he smiled a bright, winning smile.

"Yes, I'm Torie," I said.

"Come on, I'll buy you a beer," he offered.

"No thanks," I said. "I'm driving."

"Oh." He looked totally rejected.

"You can buy me a Dr Pepper," I said.

"Well, all right," he said and waved his hand in the direction of the bar.

We sat down and he ordered a beer for himself and a Dr Pepper for me. He paid the bartender, handed me my soda, and smiled. "So, what can I do for you and how did you hear of me?"

"Sylvia Pershing," I said.

He choked on his beer and sputtered a bit. I really had to learn not to speak when people were drinking. One of these days, somebody was going to choke and die and it would be all my fault.

"Ms. Pershing recommended me?" he asked.

"You could say that," I said.

"Well . . . I wasn't aware the old bat liked my services well enough to recommend me to anybody," he said.

"Really?" I asked and took a drink of my soda. Fountain Dr Pepper just wasn't the same as canned Dr Pepper. But it was better than water.

"She didn't tell you that she fired me?" he asked.

"She . . . she fired you?" I couldn't hide my surprise, unfortunately.

"Yes," he said.

"No, she didn't tell me that. How long ago did she fire you?" I asked.

"About six weeks ago."

"What was her reason for letting you go?" I asked.

"I'm not entirely sure," he said. "Let me see if I can get this right. I'm a . . . spoiled, lazy mama's boy who couldn't find my own hand if it was inserted in my—"

"I get the picture," I said and held a hand up. Well, he certainly had met and worked for Sylvia. There was no way he could have nailed her that well without having met her. I cleared my throat. "What exactly was it you failed to find for her?"

He took a drink of his beer and eyed me cautiously. "I'm not sure I should discuss that with you."

"Well, here's the deal, Mr. Walker—"

"Call me Mike."

"Mike," I said. "Sylvia is dead."

He choked on his beer yet again. I was beginning to develop a complex about it. "D-dead? As in, she's . . ."

"The opposite of living," I said. "That's right. Not breathing. In the ground."

"Well, isn't that something?" he said.

"What?" I asked.

"Nothing," he said. "I don't discuss my clients."

"Well, I'm your client now," I said. "And what I'm hiring you for is to tell me everything Sylvia hired you for."

"Sheez," he said and laughed. Then he caught the expression on my face and stopped short. "You're serious."

"Totally," I said.

"Aw, man," he said. "I just don't think it's right. You know, client confidentiality and all that."

"You're not a priest or a doctor," I said. "And I'm paying you."

He stared at the clock on the wall.

"In advance."

His eyes cut around, and the rest of his face eventually followed. "How much up front?"

"Four hundred dollars," I said.

"Make it five and I'll tell you what you want to know. I mean, she is dead, after all."

Nice to know he had scruples. "Five it is."

"I'm going to need another beer," he said and raised his hand to the bartender. Once his beer had arrived he set about telling me what I wanted to know. He somehow managed to speak and drink and still keep the toothpick safely in his mouth. "All right, about a year ago I get this phone call from this lady, this older-than-the-hills lady, and she says she needs a PI. I tell her my fees and she says she'll call me back. I figured I'd never hear from her again. But about a week later I got another phone call and I knew it was her, because, you know, she *sounded* older than anybody on the planet. She said she wanted me to come down to her place, so I went. It was big old ugly brick building in that depressed little area down in Granite County."

"It is not depressed," I said.

"Whatever," he said and shrugged. "So I go down there, and sure enough, Methuselah's wife answered the door. She took me out on the back porch because she didn't want her assistant to hear the conversation. Evidently, her assistant was this real nosy type that gets her panties in a wad over everything, and so I went out on the porch and had *tea* with this old lady."

"And?" I said. I tried very hard not to let it register on my face that I was the assistant he was referring to.

"She told me she thought somebody was trying to kill her and she wanted me to find out who it was," he said. "I told her, 'Look, why would anybody want to kill somebody as old as you? They only have to wait a few years and you'll be gone anyway.' I thought she'd get real offended by that. Sometimes I just say things without thinking, and that was one of those times, but you know, she didn't get upset. She agreed with me that she was very old and that she would probably be dead soon anyway, but she couldn't help feeling like somebody was trying to kill her. And the funny thing was that she didn't really seem to be scared or worried about it. She just wanted to know who it was."

He took a drink of his beer. "Now why do you suppose that was?"

I sat back in my chair and took a deep breath. Sylvia *had* suspected somebody was trying to hurt her. I had been right.

"Because I just came right out and told her that I wasn't a bodyguard and that I couldn't save her or help her in that respect, and she said she didn't want anybody to protect her or save her, she just wanted to know who it was that was trying to kill her."

After I found my voice I spoke. "And I'm assuming you never found out who it was, hence the reference to your lost hand."

"Exactly," he said. "I suggested the video surveillance equipment, which she did install. I followed some dead ends that she gave me, but really I found nothing significant."

"Did she say why she thought somebody was trying to kill her?"

"She said that there were some things she'd done in her life that some people might still hold a grudge about."

"That was it?" I asked. "Nothing more?"

He shrugged.

"Did she give you any names?"

"No."

"Did she ever mention anybody named Millie O'Shaughnessy?"

"No," he said.

"Well, had something happened to make her think somebody was after her? I mean, other than that stuff about grudges?"

"Said she'd heard people in the house."

"People? Plural?"

"Or a person, I'm not sure now. Evidently one night she woke up and saw somebody at the foot of her bed."

Shivers danced down my spine. "What?"

"She didn't give me details on what happened. Just that somebody was at the foot of her bed. So she hired me."

"Did she have any idea of who the person at the foot of the bed was? I mean, when was this?"

"I don't know," he said. "But I think her sister had just died at that point when she saw the person in her room. So she would have been living alone."

"Oh," I said.

"She seemed real concerned about that assistant of hers, though."

"She did?" I asked. I fought the lump that rose in my throat.

"Yeah, told me that if I ran into her I was supposed to tell her I was the plumber or something because she'd get her nose to sniffing around and get into a heap of trouble," he said. "In fact, she made it sound like her assistant could have figured the whole thing out for her, but she didn't want the assistant getting involved."

A big fat tear rolled right out of my eye before I could stop it. I swiped at it and then played with my eyelashes as if they were malfunctioning. "New mascara," I said.

His expression owed as much to disbelief as to curiosity. "So what do you want me to do?" he asked.

"I want you to give me a report of every single person who goes in and out of the Gaheimer House—which is the house you met her at—for the next few weeks. I want to know exactly what time they went in and what time they left, and I want to know every little detail down to the color of their shoelaces. Can you do that?"

He nodded. "I can take pictures, too."

"I don't care how you do it, just do it. But I'll tell you, it's a small town with people in it who are praying for something to gossip about, and by golly, you'd be the perfect candidate. So you have to make yourself invisible."

"I can do that," he said. "Believe it or not."

"Stay away from the sheriff. Stay away from the mayor."

The expression on his face suddenly dropped. "Oh, hey, this isn't going to be trouble, is it? I don't like getting mixed up with the local authorities."

"I've been mixed up with the local authorities before. It's not that bad," I said. "Just stay invisible and you won't have a problem. If the sheriff finds you snooping around, he might try to make you leave, but his bark is worse than his bite, and you're not really doing anything wrong. So just steer clear. You do that for a few weeks and it's easy money for you."

"All right," he said and finally took that damn toothpick out of his mouth. "Just one question."

"What?"

"Was Sylvia murdered?"

"It doesn't appear so," I said.

"Then why do you care about all of this?"

"That's two questions," I said.

"Oh, come on," he said. "Seriously, why does any of this matter to you?"

"I'm that nosy assistant with the wadded panties," I said.

"Oh," he said. "I really do say the stupidest things, don't I?"

"Just take pictures and log who goes in and out, and you can talk stupid forever, I won't care."

"Yes, ma'am."

Sixteen

A ll right, who's the private investigator parked outside on River Pointe Road?" Colin asked as he entered my office at the Gaheimer House the next day. I sat at my desk and just buried my face in my hands.

"That obvious?" I said. I stood immediately and walked past him to the front door.

"Hey, where are you going?"

"You entered the house with the alarm on," I said. I punched in a code and went back to my office.

"Oh," he said. "Sorry."

"What do you want?" I asked. "Because I have loads to do and I have to meet with the historical society this evening. We're voting on who should be president."

"Well, I want to know why there's a private investigator snooping around my town."

"I hired him."

"Believe it or not, I figured that much out. I want to know why."

I said nothing.

"Is this because you think Sylvia was murdered?"

"No," I said finally. "He's out there because Sylvia thought somebody was trying to kill her. That's the private investigator she hired in the first place. He's out there because I was attacked in broad daylight last weekend at the Strawberry Festival, and because Stephanie swears there's a ghost in this house. Now, since I don't believe in ghosts, that must mean that somebody was making the noises that my very levelheaded sister heard. You put all that together, and I've got Mike out there watching the house to see who comes in and out."

"Oh," he said.

"Is he that bad?" I asked.

"No," he said. "I'm trained to see that sort of thing. Most of the people in town won't notice."

"What do you mean, 'most'?"

"Well, none of my deputies have noticed, so that means Eleanore will probably figure it out, but otherwise you're safe," he said.

"That's it? You're not going to yell at me over it and make him leave?"

"No," he said. "Actually, I think it's kind of a smart thing to do."

"So you think—"

"No, I don't think Sylvia was murdered," he said. "But I do think that something is going on with this house."

"Really?" I asked and sat down. I felt a little better knowing that the sheriff was sort of on my side. It was such an unusual position for me.

"I did some questioning," he said. "Seems most of the witnesses on Sunday said they saw somebody about five foot four to five foot seven—just how tall depends on the witness—anyway, they saw this person raise a club and hit you with it."

My mouth dropped open. Then the hair stood up on my neck. Somebody *was* trying to hurt me. It hadn't been random. Funny, I wasn't nearly as frightened of the idea of somebody deliberately clubbing me in broad daylight as I was now that I *knew* somebody had deliberately clubbed me in broad daylight. Suddenly that alarm system didn't seem like enough protection.

"No other description. Seems as though the person was wearing a disguise," he said. "We found a wig and some clothes in a Dumpster."

"No way," I said. My breath came faster. The ends of my fingers tingled.

"Yes, way," he said.

"Holy sh—"

"Yes, that, too," he said.

"But wh—"

"Why?" he asked. "You tell me."

"But I—"

"Don't have a clue? Come on, tell me another one."

"No, Colin, I really don't," I said. *Think. Think.* "I mean, if somebody was just attacking *me*, I would say it was because of something I knew about this town that could harm somebody. But with what I know now about Sylvia—and the fact that her suspicions had been going on for a year—well . . . It's more convoluted than somebody attacking me because of something I know."

"Sylvia had no idea who was trying to hurt her?"

"No," I said. "You question Mike if you want. He told me that she told him she woke up one night and there was somebody standing at the foot of her bed. This was just after Wilma died, so about two years ago."

"Did the person at her bed try to hurt her?"

"I don't know. I don't think she told Mike, either," I said.

"Then it has to be some kind of connection between you and her," he said.

"What connection? There is no connection other than I worked for her for ten years and knew her all my life. Half the people in town knew her all their lives, too. The only difference is I worked for her."

Color crept into Colin's cheeks. "Her will."

I stared at him.

"You got everything," he said.

"Yes, but . . ."

"I checked with her lawyer."

"And?"

"He said Sylvia had called him about six months ago and told him that no matter what anybody said, you were the beneficiary of her will. He said she was paranoid since Wilma had died that the paperwork hadn't been done correctly. Said she kept calling to double-check that everything had switched from Wilma to you. Because Wilma was her inheritor and executor and she was Wilma's, and whoever died first, the other was to switch it to you. So after Wilma died, her lawyer said she had called and called and called making sure that everything was in order. Then about six months ago, she called and stated to him that you were the beneficiary no matter what."

There were those tears again. I reached for a tissue. "What does that mean?"

"I take it to mean that Sylvia was worried that somebody would contest the will, and she wanted you to have everything."

"But why?"

"Why what?"

"Why would anybody contest the will? I mean, *who* could contest the will? Is that what you mean by the connection between her and me? If it's the will, then only the person who thinks they should have inherited is the culprit. Is that what you're saying?"

"I'm saying most likely. There's no other connection between the two of you, right? So it has to be a disgruntled heir."

"But who? She had no children. Wilma had no children."

"Their brother did."

"He's been dead for twenty years. Maybe more."

"Yes, and his two daughters and his son are all dead as well, but those three children had five children between them," he said.

"But how could they think they would be left anything? As long as I have lived in this town, they've never set foot in it."

He shook his head.

"One of them lives just over in Wisteria, and she never came to visit."

"They all came for Wilma's funeral," he managed to add.

"Oh, gee. 'So glad you could show up for your great-aunt's funeral, here's my whole life savings.' Is that how they think that's supposed to work?"

"I guess they think it belongs to them more than it belongs to an outsider."

"Well, I've got news for you, Colin Woodrow Brooke, *they* are the outsiders," I said. "Not me. I'm the one who was here for the Pershing sisters. Nobody else."

Colin looked taken aback.

"No," I said and held my hands up. "That's not how I mean that to sound. I never once thought Sylvia was going to leave me all of this. I thought she'd leave me a few mementos and some photographs and the rest would go to charity. I really thought Sylvia would leave everything to Santa Lucia's or Catholic Charities. I never once thought I deserved to inherit this. But I did. And now when I think of Sylvia and Wilma, I don't think of their great-nieces and -nephews. I think of this town and everybody in it. This is who and what they loved. And their 'family' showed just how much they cared or thought about those two old ladies, and I don't see how any of them could even think they were entitled to their belongings."

"Well," he said as he looked out my office window, "somebody thinks so."

"How is hurting me going to help whoever it is get Sylvia's things?"

He turned to me then and crossed his arms. "Maybe they don't really care about the money. Maybe they just don't want you to have it."

"Oh, so we're dealing with juveniles."

He smiled and shook his head. "'Vengeance is mine.'"

"'Sayeth the Lord,'" I said. "Not for some greedy twit who's been waiting for that rich great-aunt to die."

"Watch your back, Torie. I'll be watching it for you," he said, "but you need to stay on your toes. Don't do anything stupid."

"Define stupid," I said.

Seventeen

Six hours later I went home for dinner. Mrs. O'Shea had cooked some weird dish with salmon. Since I despise salmon and so do my children, we all just moved it around on our plates. As soon as she headed for the shower we all ran to the kitchen and got out the peanut butter and jelly. I read Matthew a story, gave Fritz a bath in the upstairs sink—and subsequently had to change my clothes—kissed the girls, and went out the door to the historical society meeting at the Gaheimer House.

I drove, which in and of itself indicated my level of anxiety. When the weather is nice, and sometimes even when it isn't, I usually walk, but I didn't want to be alone on dark streets tonight. Besides, I was still pretty sore from what had happened to me at the festival; I got tired earlier than usual, and it was already well into the evening. It was eight o'clock when I arrived at the Gaheimer House, and a few people were waiting out on the sidewalk to be let in.

Charity Burgermeister was there with her miniature poodle, Heather. Heather wore a pink collar with rhinestones. Elmer Kolbe stood with his hands in his pockets, rocking back and forth on the balls of his feet. Elmer is the fire chief of New Kassel, and long past retirement age. Leigh Duran, Deputy Duran's wife, was in the middle of telling Charity a story about something. As soon as I pulled up, Helen Wickland came jogging across the street from the direction of her candy shop.

"Hey, everybody," I said. "Hello, Heather." The dog barked at me and bared its teeny tiny teeth. Really, I do want to know: When in the eons of time were poodles predators? Charity smiled her contagious smile and then sheepishly tapped the end of feisty little Heather's nose. My only hope was that the poodle was housebroken. Sylvia would come back from the dead to kill me if I allowed a dog to urinate on her hardwood floors.

My hardwood floors, actually. It was still too bizarre for me to comprehend.

"Come on in," I said. I didn't reset the alarm, because people would be coming in and out for the next few hours. Within minutes, ten or so members had shown up, including Eleanore Murdoch. Then my sister showed up. She wasn't a member of the historical society but, being the thoughtful person she is, realized that I might need support tonight and came of her own volition.

We were supposed to begin at eight-thirty on the nose, but we waited around for fifteen more minutes to give everybody a chance to show up. This was important, after all. Our entire slate of officers had to be decided. About forty of us were finally seated in the dining room with refreshments when I stood facing everybody and tapped on my glass. "I think we know why we are all here tonight," I said. "We need to vote on new officers. Do we have any nominations?"

"I move that the historical society be moved from the Gaheimer House," a voice in the back said. It was Eleanore, sitting all smug next to Leigh Duran. Rumbles erupted from the group, and I held a hand up to quiet everybody. Elmer raised his hand, and I gestured at him to speak.

Standing up ever so slowly, Elmer turned to face the gathering of members. "Moving the historical society is the stupidest thing I've ever heard. The Gaheimer House *is* the historical society. All of the records are in the basement, the computers are here, Torie's office is here. And Mr. Gaheimer's antique furnishings are here, and that's why people come to take tours in the first place. Which puts the revenue back into the historical society."

"That is if there's anything left in the Gaheimer House for the tourists to see by the time she sells it all off," somebody said. I glanced around to see who it was. Danny Eisenbach. I would not have thought him capable of saying such a hurtful thing, but then he has never pretended to be my best friend either. As far as I was concerned, he was just a guy who'd lived here his whole life. We moved in different circles most of the time. I never detected any hostility between us.

I held up a hand. "The only things I'm getting rid of are Sylvia's daily effects. Her toothbrush, toaster, pants, shoes. And I'm giving most of that stuff away. The Gaheimer collection stays as it is."

Elmer, who was still standing, gave me a concerned look.

Eleanore stood. "Leaving the historical society in the grips of that woman will only mean that she still has control of it. The so-called president would be a figurehead only. I think the historical society of New Kassel should be totally removed from the Gaheimer House, so that Torie will not 'inadvertently' be in charge of everything."

I was floored. I sat down in my chair, and Stephanie reached over and squeezed my hand.

"I also move that the position of chairperson for events should be taken away from her, so that we have no more incidents like the one we had with the Brown Jugs," Eleanore said.

"What reason do you have for this?" Elmer asked.

Charity then stood with Heather in tow and whirled around on Eleanore. "You're just jealous. If you can give us a reason, like one that says Torie is incapable of having these responsibilities, then we'll listen to you. Otherwise, shut your trap, Eleanore."

"Hey!" somebody said. "Eleanore is right. There shouldn't be so much power in one woman's hands."

"Oh, my Lord," Elmer said. "This isn't the bloody CIA, for crying out loud. Listen to yourselves. Power and all that crap."

Then Barbara Marina stood and said, "Why should she get all the power? She's already got all the money."

"Yeah," somebody said.

"Listen to yourselves," somebody else said. "I can't believe what I'm hearing."

Neither could I. This was the last thing I would have expected. I nearly screamed for everybody to be quiet, but the words wouldn't come out of my mouth. In fact, they couldn't come out of my mouth, because lodged deep down in my throat was a sob. I'd cry out if I yelled for everybody to be quiet, and then they would all know how much they'd hurt me, how betrayed I felt. So I just sat there in an emotional state of shock and tried hard to swallow the sobs.

Stephanie leaned in. "Do you want to leave? Let's just leave," she said.

I shook my head in the negative. Leaving would only make it appear as though I thought myself better than they were, and that was half of the issue to begin with. Besides, I didn't think I could stand up, even if I wanted to.

"Shut the hell up!" somebody screamed.

Silence engulfed the room, extinguishing all of the hateful noise like water on a fire. Everybody looked from one person to the other. Then, finally, all eyes landed on the man who had just told everybody to shut the hell up.

It was Father Bingham.

"Listen to yourselves. Listen!" he said, rising. "You're like a hungry Roman crowd at a Christian buffet. Look at her!"

He pointed at me, just as a tear ran down my face.

"She cannot help what has been willed to her."

Somebody made a disgruntled noise.

"And the basis of her inheritance hasn't got anything to do with whether or not she is fit to run this historical society. Now, I'll tell you all what. You just take the historical society. Go ahead," Father Bingham said, loosening his collar. He pushed his small round spectacles up on his nose. "Where will you take it? Does anybody here have a place where you can house all the records and the computers and the antiquities . . . and . . . and . . . collections of this society? Do you?"

The room was silent, save for Elmer, who nodded his head and said, "Hear, hear."

"We'll just start our own historical society," Eleanore said.

"Eleanore, don't be a boob," Father Bingham said. "What do you know about history? What do you know about this county? This river? The people of New Kassel?"

Nobody said a word.

"Now, I am here to tell you that there probably are a few of us in this room who could do Torie's job. But, Eleanore, you're not one of them."

"Well, I never!" she said and jumped to her feet.

"Oh, sit down and shut up," Charity said over her shoulder to Eleanore.

"Now, here's what I propose," Father Bingham began.

"With all due respect, Father," Elmer Kolbe said, "I'm the treasurer of this society, let me."

Father Bingham bowed and sat down. Elmer limped up to the front of the room. "I nominate Torie O'Shea for president of the historical society . Are there any other nominations?"

"I nominate Helen Wickland," Eleanore Murdoch said.

What a stroke of brilliance. Helen's nomination was of definite concern to me. Yes, I wanted to be president of the historical society. This is what I do best. This is who I am. And Helen, out of everybody in attendance, had the best chance of beating me. Eleanore knew this. How very shrewd. Helen was established, never ruffled any feathers, and had been a member and an officer of the historical society for years before I even came along. Plus, she was well liked and respected in the community. Her only shortcoming was that she didn't have the historical background, and that was something, at this point in time, I didn't think was going to matter much. This was going to be a popularity contest, and it seemed as though my popularity had sharply decreased now that I was wealthy.

"Helen, do you accept this nomination?" Elmer asked.

"Oh, I don't know," she said, glancing around the room. She shrugged. "Well, I suppose."

"Are there any other nominations?" Elmer asked.

"I nominate Leigh Duran," somebody said. By this point, the words were beginning to sound like a roaring lion in my ears. I could barely distinguish one person's voice from another. I had no idea who was speaking. I wasn't sure, but I thought Elmer asked if there were any other nominees.

"Runner-up will be vice president. Ladies and gentlemen, I think either way we'll have a winning team," Elmer said.

"What about the historical society?" Danny Eisenbach said. "What about where it will reside?"

"There will be no vote on that," Elmer said.

"But you can't do that!"

"Yes, I can, Danny. You people need to get something in your heads. The Gaheimer House and everything in it is privately owned. If you want to take the organization without its assets and holdings, fine. You come to me with a location for its new home, and we'll vote on it. But all that goes is the records and the computers. Mr. Gaheimer's things stay. Because they are Torie's now. Until then, don't mention it again."

Nobody had anything to say to that.

"I'm nominating myself for treasurer again," Elmer said. "Anybody else?"

Not one person raised a hand.

"Secretary?"

Stephanie raised her hand. "I would like to try."

"She's not a member!" Barbara Marina cried out. "It'll be Sylvia and Wilma all over again. A monopoly."

Stephanie pulled her checkbook out of her purse and wrote a check and handed it to Elmer. "There's my dues," she said. "I'm a member. I'd like to run for secretary. I have a degree in history. I've been a teacher for ten years and have never been arrested. I was a Girl Scout for twelve years, was on student council, and have been an officer in several organizations. There."

The room was deadly silent. Tom Petersen raised his hand and stood. "I'd kinda like to be a secretary," he said. "I'll throw in my nomination for myself."

"Let's just vote and get this over with," I said to Elmer.

Elmer nodded and handed out pieces of paper for everybody to use as ballots.

"Speeches! Speeches!" somebody cried.

I gave Elmer a disgruntled look. It was customary for the people running for an office for the first time to give a speech before the voting. In the case of running for an office that you already held, there was no need. I just wanted to vote and go home. "Well, since nobody's running against me," Elmer said, "I have nothing to say. You all know who I am anyway. I mean, you all know who all of us are. Why should we do this?"

"Because it is the custom," Father Bingham said in a soothing voice. "Let the people have their speeches."

Nobody had ever made Sylvia or Wilma give speeches.

"Fine, but I'm not doing it," Elmer said.

"I've already given my qualifications," Stephanie said.

"Mr. Petersen," Elmer said, "rise and tell us your qualifications."

Tom Petersen did so. His qualifications included winning the Granite County Bass Open. I wasn't sure what fishing had to do with any of this, but he was entitled to use whatever he saw fit to demonstrate his leadership qualities. Then it was Helen's turn.

"Well, uh, I have a degree in business from Meramec Community College. I've lived in this town my whole life. Born and raised here. My parents were born and raised here. My grandma was the first one to come here. Back in 1940. She brought two of her children with her, and the third one, my mother, was born here. I've belonged to the historical society for twenty-two years, and I've been instrumental in completing projects like the cemetery project and so forth. I would take my job as president very seriously. And I would never abuse it," she said.

I was a bit taken aback by that last statement. Helen was a dear, dear friend. Was she suggesting that I would somehow abuse being president? In fact, I thought she was acting a bit odd to begin with. She had been . . . disturbingly quiet up to this point.

"And oh yes, I was homecoming queen of 1974."

There was a slight rumble of laughter as Helen gave a fake curtsy and sat down. Leigh Duran stood and straightened her blouse and began speaking. Stephanie leaned over to me and said, "What do you think is going on here?"

I shrugged, trying desperately not to cry. She rubbed my arm.

"What was your position before?"

"Secretary, tour guide. Personal assistant to the Pershings," I whispered.

"So this is the first time this position has opened up."

I nodded. "I knew there would be people who wanted to be president, Steph. But I didn't know there were so many people who hated me."

Then it was my turn. I stood on shaky feet.

"Excuse me if I seem a bit slow-witted this evening," I said. My voice shook, and all I wanted to do was run home and cry, but I looked at Elmer and Charity and Father Bingham and a lot of faces that I knew loved me and supported me. "I really think my record stands for itself. I have served as an officer for ten years. I have been a special project coordinator for just as long. I am the one who implemented the cemetery project that Helen mentioned, along with a special exhibit on the sunken ship, *The Phantom*, and on the two great floods we've had here. I convinced Sylvia we should put all of our charts and records on the computer, something I've been busy doing for the past three years."

I stopped and looked around the room. My voice faltered and I had to swallow hard to keep going. I could not believe I had been attacked like this by these people I had known my whole life, people I had never once tried to hurt.

"Furthermore, I know more about most of your families than you do. I know the history of every building in this town. I know the history of this town and the surrounding area before there were white people living on it. But more than anything else, I love this town. I love its people. And I never thought the day would come when I would have to defend myself where it was concerned. I might not always be the most diplomatic, and I'm going to make mistakes. The Brown Jugs, obviously. But I'm good at this job. And that's all I have to say," I said and started to sit down. Then I thought of something else I wanted to add and stood up. "Just one more thing. There are moments in your life. Little moments when the clouds part and things become perfectly clear. We all have them. Some more than others. I have had plenty of them in my life. But I'll tell you the hardest lesson I've ever had to learn. Tonight, it is just as crystal clear to me as the winter sky. Money doesn't change you. It changes everybody around you."

With that I walked out of the room. Let them vote. The hell with them. Why should I care if their heritage was preserved for them or not? I mean, Elmer was right. It wasn't like this was the CIA. In the grand scheme of things in this world, this was so way down there on the scale of importance that I was ashamed of myself for even worrying about it.

So I walked right out of the building, got in my car, and drove home. I had talked myself into apathy. The numbness actually felt good.

Eighteen

When I arrived home, I walked straight through the house and out to the back porch. I stood there for a few minutes taking cleansing breaths. My chickens clucked in the darkness. They were usually asleep by now; something must have been irritating them. The leaves rustled up above, and the undeniable smell of rain hung heavy in the air.

The words from the meeting echoed in my head. *That woman.* Eleanore had called me *that woman.* When did I go from being Torie to *that woman?*

After a few minutes Rudy came out onto the porch to interrupt my trip down memory lane. I was grateful.

"How'd it go?" he asked.

"I don't want to talk about it."

"Well, Helen is here."

"Here?" I asked.

"Just knocked a second ago. Torie, what happened?"

Shaking my head in the dark, I turned and walked inside. He wouldn't have believed me even if I had told him. The whole world had gone insane, and somebody forgot to let me in on the changing of the guard. I walked into the living room with my arms crossed, ready to defend myself, but at the same time oddly disinterested.

"Torie," Helen said.

"What?"

"You won," she said.

I would have thought the news would thrill me, but, honestly, I only felt a little relieved.

"I made VP. We'll be working together," she said. "Side by side. Well, when I'm not at the candy shop. I think it'll be fun."

Just then the doorbell rang. I called for the person to come in. The door opened, and it was my sister, Stephanie. It was one of those awkward moments when nobody was sure what to say. "I . . . just came by to see if you were okay," Stephanie said, eyeing Helen.

"Well, it's not every day that one lives through a mutiny," I said.

"Oh, Torie, you're overreacting," Helen said.

"Overreacting? I was attacked tonight, Helen, and if I remember correctly, you never once spoke up in my defense," I said.

"Torie, that's not true," Helen said. "The historical society is allowed to disagree with you."

"Yes, they are, Helen. But they didn't disagree with me, Helen. They didn't disagree with one single policy or event or thing that I have done, save for hiring the damn Brown Jugs. It was not about me as a genealogist or a historian. It was personal," I said, and the tears began to fall. I liked it better when I was numb. Unfortunately, with me, the more time I have to think about something, the angrier or the more hurt I get, until I ride the wave and it goes away completely. Unfortunately, right now, I was on top of the wave.

By this point, Rudy had come into the living room, and my mother-in-law came stumbling out of the bathroom, with her hair in curlers and cold cream plastered on her face. I hadn't realized until that moment that Mrs. O'Shea had no eyebrows. Even that freak of nature could not distract me from Helen and what had just transpired.

"You cannot expect to be in your position," Helen said, "and not have to endure a few personal digs."

"I agree," I said.

"What happened tonight was way over the top," Stephanie said.

"You've taken more abuse from the mayor and not reacted like this," Helen said.

"The mayor has never claimed to be my friend. He has declared himself my enemy from the get-go. You and half those people in that room are my friends, and the other half are far from what I would call my enemies. At least that's what I thought. What happened, Helen?"

She shrugged. "People . . ."

"People what?"

"Want what they want," Helen said.

"You could have stuck up for me, Helen. I'm crushed."

"Because I ran against you?"

I stepped up close to her then. "It's not the presidency, Helen. That is not the issue. The real issue here is the Gaheimer House and the historical society in general. There's a reason Sylvia was in charge of everything, Helen. It's because she founded it, she supplied everything for it. She worked her ass off for it! Now, I don't care if I'm president or not. What I do care about is the gall of the people in that room thinking that they can move *my*—yes, that's right—*my* collections to a different location. And cut the Gaheimer House out completely, which is what it's all founded on in the first place. And totally discount all my hard work and dedication. Anyway, you can't move the historical society, because like it or not, it all belongs to me! People were ready to just take my things and run. Did anybody even think about what that sounded like? 'Oh, we don't want you to have any part of the historical society, Torie. But we still want to use all of your things.'"

"Torie, that's not true," Helen said.

"Yes it is," Stephanie said. "I was sitting there, I heard every word. That is exactly what some of the people were suggesting."

"New Kassel has a historical society because Sylvia gave it one," I said.

"Maybe we should continue this discussion during daylight

hours," Mrs. O'Shea said from behind me. "You'll wake the children."

"I tell you what, Helen. You go right on back to the meeting and you tell them that I've decided to withdraw my nomination. *And* my things. You guys just found your own little historical society. Without my help. Without my collections. Without my monetary gifts. Okay?" As soon as I said it, I knew I'd said too much. Tomorrow I would feel different, and I might have just burned a bridge. But what happened at the meeting was so bitter that it burned my heart.

"Torie, you don't mean that. Eleanore is just being a brat," she said.

"It wasn't only Eleanore speaking in there, Helen," I said.

"Torie, I was not one of them. You know I wouldn't do that to you," she said.

"No, you remained perfectly quiet throughout the whole thing," I said.

Helen backed away from me and lifted her hands in defeat. "All right," she said. "Have it your way."

Once Helen was out the door I let out a very muffled scream. In other words, I screamed without opening my mouth. Stephanie came over then and gave me a hug.

"What the hell happened tonight?" Rudy asked.

"You heard her," Stephanie said. "They ganged up on her and started accusing her of things. It was terrible."

"Well, obviously not everybody ganged up on you, or you wouldn't have won," Mrs. O'Shea said.

"Nice to know I still have some friends," I said.

"You didn't really mean what you said?" Rudy asked. "You're declining to serve and all of that?"

"I meant every word," I said. Then I remembered. I turned to Stephanie. "How did you do? Did you win?"

"Actually, I did. By one vote," she said. "I am now the corresponding secretary of the possibly defunct historical society of New Kassel, Missouri."

"Sorry," I said.

"Ahh, it's all right."

The phone rang then. Rudy answered it. "It's your mother."

"She's heard," I said.

"Really," Mrs. O'Shea said, rolling her eyes. She pulled her robe closed and turned to walk back to her room. "This town is abominable."

I made a face at the back of her head and plopped down in the recliner. "I don't want to talk to her," I said to Rudy, who was waiting patiently with the telephone in his hand. "Tell her I'll call her in the morning."

"All right," Rudy said and shrugged.

"I'm going to go," Stephanie said. "I've got a doctor's visit early in the morning."

"All right," I said. "Thanks for everything."

"Sure thing," she said. "I locked up and set the alarm for you."

"Oh, good," I said. I had totally forgotten.

As she left, Rudy walked into the living room and sat down on the piano bench on the other side of the room. Fritz ran up and scratched at my legs. He wanted up on the couch but was far too short-legged to get himself there without help. I picked him up and began petting him.

"You . . . Torie . . . I . . . This is too surreal," Rudy said.

"Tell me about it," I said. "I couldn't believe it, Rudy. I could not believe the venom."

"No, I mean, you can't give up the historical society."

"Watch me."

"Torie, this is all you know!"

"Maybe I'll learn something new. Isn't that what Collette is always after me to do? And your mother? They'll be happy."

"But it's who you are," he said.

"Well, people change."

"Sylvia would not be happy to know that she willed you everything and now you're just going to . . . to . . . what exactly?"

"I don't want to talk about it, Rudy. I just want to be left alone. I need to calm down."

After a long pause he finally raised his hands and said, "Fine." With that he walked out of the room. As I heard his steps on the staircase, I nestled Fritz even closer and reached for the television remote control.

Nineteen

I took my mother out to brunch the next day at Pierre's Bakery. I couldn't tell if the stares and gawking that we were having to endure were real or imagined. The town was used to seeing my mother out and about, so it wasn't like when we went to St. Louis and people tripped over themselves looking at the lady in the wheel-chair. Either the unusual attention that the two of us were getting was my imagination or the entire town had heard what transpired last night. I was betting on the last one.

"I'm just saying that you should take more time to consider what you're doing," Mom said. "What will you do?"

"Well, I'm thinking about going back to school. Maybe I could get a teaching job like Stephanie."

"You hate children."

"I do not hate children. I have three of my own and adore the ground they walk on!"

"Okay, you hate other people's children."

"Well . . . okay, maybe."

"So teaching probably wouldn't be a good job."

"Maybe I could get a research job. Like at a university."

"Oh, they're just handing those jobs out left and right."

"I don't really need to get a job, Mom. I have more money than I ever thought I would have, and I have an income from the rental properties that surpasses anything Rudy brings home. Maybe I'll just do some volunteer work," I said and took a bite of my pastry. "Hey, maybe I'll do nothing."

"You'd die within a week."

I shrugged. "I don't hate other people's children. Just the ones that think they're the boss. Well, and not even those, because then I'd have to hate my own daughter."

"I'm really sorry about last night," Mom said.

"Eh, don't worry about it," I said.

Colin stepped into the bakery then, clanking the cowbell on the door as he came through. He pulled up a chair, leaned over and kissed my mother, and then said, "Did you get me anything?"

I handed him a white paper bag. He opened it and smiled. "Well, Torie, I think I've struck out on the pictures."

"What pictures?"

"I've been going through all of the pictures taken at the Strawberry Festival, including the ones from your camera. I can't get a clear shot of the perp who attacked you. We do have some skin and fibers from the wig we found discarded, but with nothing to compare them to, they're kind of useless."

"We have to have a suspect first," I said.

"Right."

I took a drink of my tea and glanced around the room.

"I heard about last night," he said. "Angry mob."

"It was . . . You know, I don't care. Really, there are starving people in the world, people who have land mines in their front yards, people who have dirt for floors. Who really gives a crap what happens to some dinky little historical society in some podunk depressed town?"

"Podunk?" Colin asked.

"Depressed?" Mom asked.

I shrugged. "Maybe Mrs. O'Shea is right. Maybe Rudy and I should move up to St. Louis County. You know, back to civilization."

"Oh, my God, it's worse than I thought," Mom said.

"What?"

"You're agreeing with your mother-in-law. Do you hear yourself?"

"I'm only saying that it's really pretty trivial. All of it."

Just then Sally Huber made her way to our table. I now owned Sally's house. "Hi," she said.

I sat up straighter and wiped my mouth. "Hello, Sally."

"I hate to interrupt," she said and waved at my mother and Colin.

"No, go ahead," I said.

"Um . . . I was wondering if you could have Rudy come over and check the leak in the basement."

"Sure," I said. "Tonight when he gets in."

"Thanks," she said. "Well, you all have a nice day."

"You, too."

My mother was staring at me when I finished my tea. "What?"

I wasn't sure exactly what she was thinking, but clearly something had upset her. "Nothing," she said. As much as I hate it when parents do that, I'm just as guilty of it, so there wasn't a whole lot I could say about her saying, "Nothing."

"Are you going to work today?" Colin asked, eyeing the two of us suspiciously.

"Yeah," I said. "Regardless of what happens, I still need to finish going through Sylvia's things."

"How's that going?" Mom asked.

"Pretty good," I said. "A little sad."

"Are you going to keep any of her things for yourself?"

"A few things. Some personal things. Like her and Wilma's baby shoes, and most of her photographs. A few pieces of jewelry . . ." I frowned.

"What's wrong?" Mom asked.

"Have either one of you seen Sylvia's ring?"

"What ring?"

"That white gold sapphire ring. She used to wear it on special occasions. I can't find it anywhere," I said.

"Did you bury it with her?"

"No," I said. "The only ring she was wearing was the one Hermann Gaheimer gave her. And I buried her with one of her rosaries. I've been looking all over for that ring. I mean, it's not that valuable, but it was my favorite thing of hers, and I wanted to keep it."

"Why would we have seen it?"

"Because I think I wore it once. I mean, I know I was going to wear it. I can't remember if I actually did. I just thought maybe you guys would remember it," I said.

"No," Mom said, "but I'll keep an eye out for it."

"Hey, any word from your PI?" Colin asked.

"I should hear from him today." I picked up the tab and looked at it, then put money down to cover it. "Okay," I said. "Well, the company was wonderful. I'm off to work."

With that I left the bakery, all eyes watching me as I went. I didn't really care. I walked down to the Gaheimer House, head down, thinking about what I would do today. Stephanie wouldn't be in, and I had quite a few things to try to finish.

Before I knew it, I was at the house and letting myself in. I should finish the bedrooms today. Then the only things left would be Sylvia's office and Wilma's room. Stephanie had already taken care of the kitchen and the bathrooms and quite a few boxes of possessions for me. The first thing I did was grab a Dr Pepper and boot up my computer. I dashed off a few e-mails, including one to Laura James, the genealogist in Iowa, asking if she had any information on the O'Shaughnessy family of Dubuque. I then posted a few items on GenForum. I was still very curious about Millie O'Shaughnessy. Besides, after yesterday's fiasco, finding out who she was would be a welcome distraction.

A few hours later I was upstairs in Sylvia's room, packing up the last of her things. There were several boxes for charity and a single box of possessions for me to take home and keep. Among the items in that box was a scarf that Sylvia always wore, a sheer emerald green that glistened when the light hit it. I had also kept a few sets of her hair clips, a few pieces of jewelry, her hairbrush set, her sewing basket, and her baby shoes. Now I just had Wilma's things to go through. When Wilma died, Sylvia shut the door to her sister's room and never entered it again. Wilma's things wouldn't be as tough for me, though. She'd been dead longer, and Wilma had meant something entirely different to me than Sylvia had.

There was a buzz at the door, and I went downstairs to answer it. "Elmer," I said, opening the door wide. "Come in."

"I just came by to say how sorry I was about last night," he said as he stepped across the threshold.

"Not your fault. In fact, you were quite the Sir Percival."

"I . . ." he said. He scratched his head. "I heard you weren't going to take the job."

"That's right."

"Torie, you can't do that. Think about New Kassel."

"What about it?"

"If you quit . . . I mean, our history is all that keeps this town afloat. Tourism is the only thing this town has."

"The shops will be here, regardless."

"Yes, but . . . you know as well as I do that it's the historical society that funds things like the Strawberry Festival," he said.

I shrugged. "Didn't seem to bother anybody last night."

"No, you're wrong. It bothered twenty-two out of the thirty-eight people who were here. That's how many voted for you," he said.

"Oh, well, that only leaves sixteen disgruntled historical society members," I said.

"I'd say half of those sixteen weren't thinking clearly. Half of them probably didn't even realize the connection between the historical society and our tourism," he said.

"Oh, okay. They just hate me."

"No, that's not what I meant. You know, Torie, what the power of a crowd can do," he said. "They get caught up in what's going on and don't think clearly. I betcha half of them are ashamed this morning."

"Whatever," I said.

"Torie—"

"I really appreciate what you did for me last night," I said. "And the fact that you're not stupid like so many other people are. You remained levelheaded. Really, I do. But I need time to think."

"Okay, good," he said. "I can live with that. Just don't make any rash decisions. And it's not just for the town, Torie. It's for Sylvia. And for you. I've watched you grow up. You're like a niece to me."

"Thanks," I said and gave him a big old hug.

"I gotta get going," he said. "I'm getting a new Dalmatian today."

"Oh, joy," I said. Dalmatians are beautiful, but quite frankly, they have more energy than any living creature should be allowed to have.

He left, and I went into my office. I picked up the phone and called the St. Vincent de Paul Society to come and get some of the boxes that I had set aside for charity. They agreed to come by later in the week. Then I sat down and checked my e-mail.

I had received an answer from my contact in Iowa. It read:

Dear Torie,

I checked the white pages for Dubuque, and there are a few O'Shaughnessy families living in the area. However, there were none in the entire county prior to 1930. That's not to say there weren't any in the whole state. Now, I was wondering if you could return the favor and look something up for me? I'm looking for a Bridget Orr, who arrived in St. Louis about 1935 or 1940. Actually, I have a whole list of names, but I'll just do one at a time. If you could see if you come up with that name on any of the St. Louis records you have access to, I'd appreciate it. Feel free to ask me for any other favors.

Laura James

I typed a response, saying I'd be happy to check what I could for her. Downstairs in the basement, I actually had the "white pages" for the city of St. Louis for the years 1922 through 1929 and then again from 1937 to 1949. They had been a donation to the historical society a few years back. I could check those with no trouble, but I'd have to go down to the library to check for marriages and other records.

I glanced at my watch and wondered when I'd hear from Mike Walker. If I didn't hear something soon, I'd give him a call and check in.

Pulling the postcard out of my purse, I studied it a moment. Little Millie O'Shaughnessy must have been just passing through Iowa. On her way to where? And why did she feel the need to send Sylvia a postcard? It had to have been written by an adult, anyway, because Millie wouldn't have been old enough to write, much less write a sentence in that sort of neatly defined script.

Also, how did Sylvia end up with the other photograph of her? That wasn't a postcard, so Sylvia either had the picture mailed to her in an envelope or had taken the photograph herself. I set the second photograph of the girl, the one that indicated her identity, on my desk and began to study it.

In the photograph, Millie stood on a street corner, waving at the photographer, giving a shy smile. A woman dressed in a dark suit with a big hat was on the corner with her, turning and looking back over her shoulder. Clearly, she was an unexpected subject in the picture. By the look on her face, you could almost see her own embarrassment at being caught in the girl's photograph. The length of the woman's skirt indicated to me that the Roaring Twenties were over and the more conservative thirties had been ushered in. Or at the very least, the photograph had been taken somewhere between 1928 and 1932.

I took my magnifying glass and tried to see what was written on one of the windows on the street. VanDyke Printers. Above and behind the girl's head was a street sign. One street was Wayne Junction. I couldn't make out the cross street clearly, but what I could see was "wn Ave."

I was fairly certain there was no street in St. Louis called Wayne

Junction, but who knew what streets used to be called? Now all I had to do was find a city that had a street named Wayne Junction. Past or present.

I wasn't sure if I was encouraged by this or discouraged. At one time, I would probably have hung my head and cried. But not now. Not with the Internet. God bless the Internet.

Twenty

I yawned and stretched and immediately wished I hadn't. The bruised flesh rubbed across my rib cage and caused a very unpleasant sensation. I reached for the prescription-strength ibuprofen and the OxyContin and washed them down with Dr Pepper. My kidneys were going to crystallize.

Instead of searching for Wayne Junction, I began my search for Bridget Orr for my contact in Iowa. She had done me a favor; it was only fair that I return it. In fact, I did find a Bridget Orr listed in the 1937 phone directory. Whether it was the same Bridget Orr that Ms. James was looking for, I hadn't a clue. I would pass it on and see if she wanted me to back it up with anything else. I e-mailed Laura James and told her what I had found.

I glanced at my watch and realized why my stomach was grumbling. It was going on 6:00 P.M. Still no word from Mike Walker. A small flower of anxiety bloomed in my chest as I picked up the phone and dialed his cell phone. I got his voice mail.

Then I heard it. Footfalls on the stairs. I was not about to let this prankster out of the house without learning his identity once and for all. I jumped up out of my chair and ran into the living room. "Stay right where you are!" I called out. You always wonder how people manage to die in bizarre ways. You know, the Darwin Awards. You hear them on the news. My favorite was the guy who tossed an electric cable into a lake to electrocute the fish and then walked into the lake to retrieve the fish without unplugging the current. Well, believe me, charging out of my office right out through the living room and sitting room and heading for the stairs was probably the stupidest thing a person could do. In fact, as I was rounding the corner, I flashed on my headline for the Darwin Award.

CRAZY GENEALOGIST RUNS HEADLONG INTO ASSAILANT, DIES OF CONCUSSION

But I couldn't help it. I was incensed. I was so angry at whoever was playing games that I let my stupidity get the better of me. I heard a door shut and something fall over. I took the stairs two at a time and only thought momentarily of how winded I was when I reached the top. Maybe I would die of a heart attack. Maybe I should start exercising. Especially if I was going to make a habit out of chasing ghosts up the stairs in the Gaheimer House.

When I reached the top of the stairs I noticed the door to Wilma's room was slightly cracked. It had been shut tight. I glanced around for something to use as a weapon. I had the prowler cornered; I needed to follow through. One of those brass coatracks stood in the corner. Yeah, that'd be great.

I picked it up. It weighed a ton. I could no more wield this than I could a tree trunk. While I was standing there in the hallway, I glanced at the phone and intercom system that hung on the wall. I picked up the phone, dialed 911, and told Deputy Newsome that I had the perp cornered and he should get somebody over here.

"You may as well come out!" I called to the unseen bad guy. "Police are coming. You're trapped."

Of course, he didn't come out. I mean, that's like when the clerk at the post office asks you if you're mailing anything potentially hazardous, breakable, flammable, etc. Like, if you were mailing anthrax, you'd come out and say, "Oh, yeah, there's anthrax in there." Still, I felt stupid standing there and not saying anything.

Where was Sylvia's baseball bat when I needed it? In fact, I hadn't seen it in days. Not since . . . the Strawberry Festival.

Colin must have been right down the street because he literally burst through the door, splitting the frame, with his gun drawn. "Torie, come down from there!" he shouted.

I raised my hands, as if I were the suspect, and passed him on the stairs as he was coming up. "He ran into Wilma's room."

"Which one is that?"

"Oh, the second on the left."

I heard him kick Wilma's door open, and I froze on the stairs. I listened. Nothing. A few moments went by, and then Colin came out of Wilma's room and looked down at me. "There's nobody in here."

"What?" I said and ran back up to the room. "Did you check in the closet?"

"Of course I checked in the closet. I'm a cop."

"Well, what about under the bed? Men don't think of that too often."

"I checked under the bed, Torie."

"The windows?"

"Shut. Locked from the inside."

I stared in disbelief. "That is not possible!" I shrieked.

He shrugged. I went into the room and looked in all the places he'd said he'd looked, just because I didn't believe he'd actually done it. If he had done it, he would have found something. Somebody ran up those steps and into this room. He had to still be here.

Colin came in the room behind me.

"Did you check in the drawers?" I asked. He gave me an incredulous look. "Maybe he's small boned."

"Or a contortionist?"

"Yeah, you never know," I said, pulling out the drawers. No, no Harry Houdini inside. I sat down on the edge of Wilma's bed and put my head in my hands.

Colin sat down next to me. "Are you sure you heard a person? Maybe it's a squirrel on the roof."

I glared at him.

"Old houses make weird noises," he reminded me.

"There was somebody here. And people don't just walk through walls!"

"Maybe there's access to the attic in this room," he said.

"Maybe," I said.

Colin opened the closet and looked up at the ceiling. Nothing. No door to the attic. He shrugged. "I'm out of ideas."

"Wait," I said. "People don't walk through walls."

"Right. Physics."

I snapped my fingers. "But what if the walls move?"

"What?"

I ran to the closet. "Sylvia used to tell me all the time about how some of the older homes had secret rooms. You know, like for Indian attacks."

"Indians? In Missouri?"

"Well, the Gaheimer House would have been built long after the Native American 'threat' would have passed in this area. But some people, especially if they were wealthy or lived out in rural areas, would build a safe room."

"You mean, like a panic room."

"Yeah, only without Jodie Foster. Exactly. Sometimes wealthier people had these rooms just to keep their treasures in, so that if they were robbed by bandits or what have you, their real wealth would be safe."

"Did you say bandits?" Colin said. "Do people really use that word?"

"Look," I said and moved Wilma's clothes aside. "At one time New Kassel was a remote stop along the railroad between St. Louis and Memphis. I think there was this house, and the Queen house, which is now Eleanore's, and a few others. The railroad often brought some unsavory people with it."

"You need a flashlight?" he asked and handed me his.

"Thanks."

I ran the yellow beam of the flashlight along the wall of the closet. Nothing. Then I turned and moved the hanging clothes all back the other way and faced the north wall of the closet. There, as big as you please, was a panel.

"Colin," I said, "I think I found our secret room."

Colin leaned his head into the closet. "You're joking!"

"No," I said.

"Don't touch that panel," he said. "I'll have it dusted for prints."

"Well, remove the panel, then," I said. "Don't you have gloves or something?"

Colin took a pen from his pocket and popped one corner of the panel. Then he pulled out a handkerchief and slid it aside. I flashed the light into the dark space. A staircase led downward. "It's not a room at all," I said. "It's a way out."

Twenty-One

Wooden steps led down into a pit of total blackness. Colin and I said nothing for the longest time. We just stared down into the corridor and then at each other. "I really didn't expect to find anything," I said. Only in the desperate recesses of my mind had I been holding out hope that I would find something behind these walls.

"Me neither," Colin said, "but it makes sense. All the noises that you've heard, and Stephanie has heard, and then never being able to find anything. The perp was disappearing down these stairs. By the time you or the police got upstairs, there was nothing here."

"A ghost," I said.

"Like a ghost."

"And Sylvia," I said. "The person at the foot of her bed."

"Poor woman."

"But wait. If Sylvia knew there was a secret stairwell, then she would have known how her assailant got in, and she would have known how the person at the foot of her bed got in. What would have been the point in hiring a private investigator? She would have just called you and told you to come over and watch the panel in the closet."

Colin shrugged. "You got a point. Makes no sense."

"Is it possible she didn't know about this passage?"

"Water under the bridge now. We have to deal with why the perp is doing what he's doing."

"I know. What's the point?"

"To make you look like you're losing your mind?" he said. "Although he really didn't have to go to these lengths to prove his point."

I jabbed him. "Funny."

"The perp could also be stealing things. A few items at a time."

I thought about Sylvia's ring. "That's pretty silly, though. I mean, unless you know antiques, I don't see how that would be very lucrative. Plus, it's not like he could carry a sideboard or a chest down these stairs."

We were both quiet again.

"How long are we going to stand in the closet?" Colin said.

"Well, aren't you going to go after him?"

"He's long gone," he said, stepping out of the closet. "Besides, I'm not going down there without backup."

"I'll back you up."

"Thanks, but no thanks. I also don't want to disturb the evidence. Something you don't think of when you go off on one of your tears."

"Yeah, whatever," I said. Then, under my breath, "I still get my man, or woman. Usually."

Colin called for backup while I stood there with the flashlight, staring down the steep, dark, dank flight of stairs. Who could know about this? I hadn't even known about it, and I'd worked in this house for years and lived in this town my whole life.

"Got any idea who would know about this secret staircase?" Colin asked.

"I was just wondering that myself," I said.

"Guess there's no way to just ask people," he said. "Then they'd know we were on to them."

"Elmer probably knows about it. I mean, any of the older residents who are interested in history might know, but then you would think they would have mentioned it at some point," I said. "Plus, if Sylvia or Wilma didn't know about it, I don't see how anybody else could."

"Maybe nobody knows about it," he said. "Except the perp."

"Possible."

"I think we should put a guard here and catch him the next time he tries to come through," he said.

"What if he doesn't try it again? I mean, I almost caught him this time."

"I can still place a guard," he said. "Won't hurt."

A few minutes passed before a very tired-looking Deputy Duran finally showed up. He walked into the room and nodded at me. I waved.

"Duran, what you see here, you cannot talk about to anybody," Colin said.

"All right," Deputy Duran said and swallowed.

"If it leaks, it could blow our only chance of catching the guy."

"I understand, sir."

"You call Crime Scene Unit?"

"Yeah."

"I want the panel dusted, and I want the stairs dusted for foot and shoe prints."

"I'll be outside," I said.

"Outside?" Colin asked.

"There has to be an exit," I said. "You think these stairs dump in the basement or to another access outside altogether?"

"Good question," he said. "I'll go with you."

We made it to the bottom of the stairs to my office in record time. Adrenaline was pumping, and I felt fairly invincible. We were going to catch this jerk or I'd know the reason why. I grabbed my cell phone from my desk and dialed Rudy to tell him I might be a little late coming home. Then, while I was at it, I phoned my private investigator once more.

"Who are you calling now?" Colin asked.

"Mr. Walker. My private investigator," I said. "Don't you think it's weird he hasn't called me or your office to see what is going on in the house? He should be out there somewhere watching the house and seeing the flurry of official activity."

We stepped out onto the back porch.

"Maybe he fell asleep," he said.

"Great," I said. "If he's sleeping, his butt is fired."

"I don't see an access out here," Colin said as we walked around the house. "It has to come out through the basement."

"Well, let's not act like we're looking for an outside exit to a secret stairwell or people will know we're up to something," I said. Mr. Walker's phone was still ringing. "I'm going to leave him one more message. I knew I shouldn't have paid him in advance."

"You paid him in advance?" Colin asked, as if I were the most gullible person on the planet.

"I was desperate."

"Wait," Colin said. "Do you hear that?"

I heard something vaguely, in the distance, like a song on a music box. Then it stopped. Mr. Walker's voice mail kicked in. "Mike, it's Torie. Where the hell are you? Call me."

Colin turned to me then with an expression that gave me serious goosebumps. "Dial Mr. Walker's number again."

"Okay," I said. I hit the speed dial. The music started playing.

"It's coming from the garden," he said and pointed.

"What is it?"

"*Take me out to the ball game,*" he sang as he walked toward the garden. "*Take me out with the crowd.*"

Just as I was about to berate him for singing—off-key, no less—at a time like this, I realized what I was hearing. Mr. Walker's cell phone. Colin pulled his gun and motioned for me to stay put. He rounded the strawberry plants and the little patch where corn would grow tall in August. Then he knelt down on one knee and spoke quickly into his radio. He walked briskly back toward me and took my phone and pushed the hang-up button.

In the distance, the music stopped playing.

"What?" I said.

"It's your private detective," he said and kept walking.

"Is he . . . is he dead?"

"Not yet," he said. "But if he lives, I'll stop fishing."

I clasped my hand over my mouth and took a step backward. Somebody had attacked me at the Strawberry Festival, and somebody was utilizing a secret stairwell inside the Gaheimer House that I hadn't even known about. Now somebody had attacked and nearly killed a private investigator that nobody was supposed to know was on the job.

Now I was afraid.

Twenty-Two

The crowd had gathered, the one that always gathers anytime there's an ambulance and the possibility of seeing a dead body is imminent. I've seen dead bodies. Really, I don't see what all the hoopla is about.

The Wisteria General Hospital ambulance whisked away Michael Walker. The crowd would have to be disappointed today. Shucks, he was still alive. Colin stepped toward me as I watched the ambulance round the corner and head toward Wisteria. "We're not telling the papers what happened. We're telling them a drunk wandered into the garden and fell and hit his head."

I nodded and hugged myself close. "What did happen?"

"He was bludgeoned," he said. "At least that's my call."

"If he dies, it's my fault," I said. "I hired him."

"Torie, don't think like that."

"Was he . . . bludgeoned right there in the damn backyard, Colin?"

"No," he said. "Looks like he was attacked elsewhere and collapsed there trying to get to the house."

"Why didn't he use his cell phone?"

"He might have," Colin said. "Maybe he couldn't talk. I don't know."

"What's the point in having a cell phone if it doesn't save your life?"

"Take it easy, Torie. Don't get yourself all worked up."

"Well, I *am* worked up, Colin! I can't help it, I am."

I glanced around the crowd and saw the mayor standing there talking with my mother-in-law. Their heads were together as if they didn't want anybody else to hear what they were saying. Hands gestured in my direction. I looked up at the sky and wished for the millionth time that Sylvia had, indeed, been immortal. I wished she had never died. I wished she had never left me her fortune. I wished she had never left me the Gaheimer House. I wished she had never left me shards of her life to decipher.

I had the mother-in-law from hell staying in my home. I didn't need anything else on my plate.

"I gotta go," I said.

"Where are you going?" Colin asked.

"Home," I said. "Before I hurt something. Or somebody."

"Hey," Colin said as I turned to go. "Talk to your husband. You're leaving him out of the loop."

"Oh, did he say that?"

"No, I can tell. You guys are never like this."

I shrugged. "Can't help it. He brought this on himself."

"Don't alienate the one person who knows you better than anybody and still loves you," Colin said.

I ignored him and walked all the way back to my house with my head hanging. This was too much. I always juggled a thousand things at once. I thrived on chaos and deadlines. Not this time. My mind was cloudy, my heart heavy, my shoulders aching.

When I entered my house, Mrs. O'Shea was there. So Rudy had already heard the news about a stranger from out of town stumbling through the backyard of the Gaheimer House and nearly killing himself on a rock.

In fact, they were still discussing it when I opened the door. I could hear the voices coming from the kitchen. My mother-in-law's voice was unmistakable, especially when she was riled. "I don't care what that sheriff says," Mrs. O'Shea said. "That man was beaten."

"How would you know?" Rudy asked.

"Because Mayor Castlereagh saw the man as they were lifting him onto the stretcher. Even his arms were black and blue," she said. "Now, I am going to ask you one more time, Rudolph. What kind of town are you raising my grandchildren in?"

"New Kassel is a wonderful town," he said. "Every town has its problems. Every town has violence. And they are my children first, your grandchildren second. Don't forget that."

Mrs. O'Shea made some dismissive noise. I couldn't see them, and I didn't want them to know I was there just yet, so I stood in the doorway of my living room with my hand on the door. That way I could pretend I had just entered and shut the door if they discovered I was standing there.

"The mayor says otherwise."

"Mom," he said, "there was a college professor killed here last year while working on that shipwreck that happened back a long time ago."

"What about that man in the abandoned building?"

"That was ruled an accident."

"And the man floating in the river? Torie's uncle, I believe?"

"He slipped. Another accident," he said. "Mom, what do you think you're going to accomplish by this discussion?"

"I think you should move," she said. "That's all."

Silence.

"Back to St. Louis County," she added.

I couldn't stand it anymore. "Yeah, why don't you go on back to St. Louis County, Rudy?"

"Torie," he said, coming around the corner to stand in the living room. "I didn't hear you come in."

"How could you with Motor Mouth in there?"

"Torie, stop," he said with his hands up.

"No, you stop," I said. "She's been after us to move out of this town since we got married. You want to know why? Because this is my territory. She can't control us here. And she can't stand it."

"Torie, stop!"

"Oh, fine, who cares, anyway?" I turned and stormed out of the house, slamming the door behind me.

Great, I'd just alienated myself from my own house. I couldn't go to my mother's because she'd already made it clear that I couldn't stay there as long as Mrs. O'Shea was in town. At one time I would have gone to Helen's, but now I felt weird about that. After yesterday's events.

And so I walked.

I walked until I found myself staring up at the entrance to the Santa Lucia Catholic church. The church I was married in is white sandstone, with stained glass windows framing the large wooden doors. One large round stained glass window peers down from above the doors like a giant eyeball watching the townsfolk of New Kassel. I pulled on the heavy wooden door, knowing it would be open. All the churches in New Kassel are left unlocked at all times—something you won't find up in stupid old St. Louis County.

The wooden pews spread forward in perfect rows, two rows for each of the Stations of the Cross plaques hanging along the walls. I sat down for a moment, just to breathe, but it didn't make me feel any better. I was still too scared and too angry. I got up and walked over to the confessional and opened the door. I knelt at the window.

"Hello? Anybody there?" I asked.

A rustling noise came from the other side of the mesh window. "Yes, I'm here." It was Father Bingham. If I hadn't known better, I would have said he had fallen asleep waiting for sinners.

"Father, forgive me, for I have sinned," I said.

"And what sins do you wish to confess?"

"Well . . . Father, forgive me, for I am not Catholic."

Silence. Then, finally, "Forgiven," he said. "Anything else?"

"Oh, Father," I said, "I have made such a mess of things."

Surprisingly, he didn't push me. He didn't treat the confessional like an assembly line for sinners. He sat patiently and waited for me to speak.

"I . . . Father, it's Torie. Can I see your face?"

"Certainly," he said. I heard him open the door and come around to the door on my room. He entered and sat down in the chair opposite the mesh window. I stood and then sat in the other chair. A small round table with a candle and some leaflets stood between us. "What can I do for you?" he asked.

I put my face in my hands. "I hate my mother-in-law. There, I said it. I despise the woman. She is so mean to me. She has hated me since the day she met me. She doesn't think I'm good enough for Rudy. She thinks everything I do is trivial—well, it is sort of trivial, but that's beside the point. She's hateful, narcissistic, manipulative . . . she is poison, Father. Absolute poison."

He said nothing.

"Aren't you going to tell me what a terrible person I am?"

"No," he said.

"I want her to go away and never come back. I literally don't care if I ever see this woman again. I mean, I don't want anything bad to happen to her, but I wish she'd go away. There's just one problem. My husband happens to love his mother. which drives me insane because I don't understand how he can love somebody who hates his wife."

"You want him to dislike her as much as you do?" he asked.

"No, I just want him to choose me! I feel so betrayed, Father. If his mother was nice to me and I still hated her, that would be one thing. But she is evil. Pure evil. Satan lives in the follicles of her hair!"

"Torie, really," he said. "I think you're overreacting a bit."

"Okay, fine, but you see my dilemma. The fact that Rudy still loves her and overlooks her offenses makes me feel like he doesn't love me. I mean, how can you love somebody who hates your spouse?"

"Some mothers have trouble letting go," he said.

"Bah! That's a cop-out line if I ever heard one. You know from the minute you give birth to your children that you're raising them to give to somebody else. If you don't know that, then you're in serious denial."

"Maybe she feels the same way."

"What do you mean?"

"Maybe she feels like you hate her and she can't understand how her son could possibly love somebody who hates his mother."

His suggestion stopped me dead, but it didn't take me long to rally. "Yes, but *I* am not the one who insulted her first. She insulted me, to my face, the day we met!"

"You're a threat. Obviously."

"So that gives her the right to be so mean to me?"

"I didn't say that."

"Well, what are you saying, Father? Because so far, you're not helping me much."

"Jesus said to love your enemies."

"Well, and thus you'll notice I don't listen to him too often."

"Torie," he said and leaned forward, "where's the humanity in loving those who love you? That's the easy job. But loving those who do not love you is the true test of a humanitarian. A decent human being."

A tear rolled down my face before I could stop it.

"You passed that test with Sylvia," he went on.

"What are you talking about?"

"Sylvia was the most cantankerous, hateful woman who walked the streets of New Kassel and beyond," he said. "Yet you loved her."

"That's different," I said and swiped at another tear.

"How is it different?"

"Because Sylvia was a good person underneath all of that gruff exterior. She helped people," I said.

"She also hurt people. She controlled people's lives. Sylvia couldn't stand for anybody to own any property in this town because then she couldn't control what happened on it," he said. "You know this. This is not news to you, Torie."

"No," I said, refusing to listen.

"She was overly critical of you. And of everybody. Yet you still loved her. You forgave her those things," he said. "Why can't you extend that same courtesy to your mother-in-law?"

I was sobbing now. Tears rolled down my face faster than I could wipe them away. I felt like such a jerk.

"Because you refuse to see your mother-in-law as a person. You refuse to look past it all to see the person underneath. Just as you looked past Sylvia's shortcomings and found the good person—the person who gave to charity and left you everything—so you would find good things in your mother-in-law, too. And even if you didn't, you should feel pity for her, Torie. Love her anyway. For she is much more miserable than you."

I sat listening to his words through my sniffling and sobbing. He handed me a Kleenex, and I wiped my eyes and blew my nose.

"Why did Sylvia have to leave me everything?" I asked.

"Because you are strong," he said. "If you weren't, she would have left it to somebody else."

I chuckled at that. Oh, real strong. Sitting across from Father Bingham crying so hard my eyes were swollen and my Kleenex was soaked. Oh, exactly the person I'd leave a fortune and a world of responsibility to.

"And because she loved you," he said, "through all of the hatefulness and spitefulness. She managed to learn to love somebody other than herself and Wilma."

"Ooooh," I said and began crying again.

"There, there," he said.

"I feel like such a jerk," I sobbed.

"Don't."

I took a deep breath and stood up. "Well, don't I have to say a bunch of Hail Marys or something?"

"No, that's for club members only," he said and smiled. His blue eyes twinkled. "Besides, your enlightenment is enough payment for the sin committed. Which is why we confess in the first place."

"Thank you," I said.

He stood then and surprised me by giving me a big hug. "You'll be all right," he said. "There is nobody I would trust this town to more than you."

"Thanks again," I said. I stepped out of the confessional and out of the church into the purple of dusk. Now I had to go home and face Rudy and his mother. I had to go home sometime. Might as well be now.

Twenty-Three

A s I was walking home, Colin pulled up in his sheriff's car and flashed his lights at me. I stopped and waited for him to pull over. I was going to feel really foolish if Rudy had sent out Colin to find me. But as my stepfather stopped his car, the look on his face suggested this was business, or at least something far more serious than a worried husband. Immediately my mind flashed on Mike Walker being carried away on the stretcher.

"Get in," he said.

I walked in front of his car to the passenger side and got in. "Anything on Walker?"

"Surprisingly, they're saying that he's stabilized," he said. His words sent a wave of relief through me. "He's going to be in a world of hurt for a week at least. He lost a lot of blood and has a concussion and about eight broken bones, but evidently he has a fairly hard head. I think he's going to live."

"So you're going to give up fishing?" I asked.

"Not on your life."

"I knew you didn't mean it," I said.

"No, that's how convinced I was that he would die."

"You're insufferable."

"I've got something to show you," he said.

"What?"

"First, I need to tell you that Leigh Duran is in the hospital," he said.

Leigh had suffered several miscarriages, so that was the first thing that sprang to my mind, but as far as I knew she wasn't pregnant. "What happened?"

"She . . . tried to commit suicide."

"What?" I said. "Oh, that's horrible. What about Duran?"

"Obviously, I let him go to her," he said.

"No, I mean, is he all right?"

"I guess that all depends how his wife is," he said.

"Is she . . . I mean, is she expected to live?"

He shrugged. "I honestly don't know."

"Does Duran . . . does he know why she tried to kill herself?"

"I don't know. But me personally, I think it's over the miscarriages. She's been pretty set on having a baby, and so far nothing has happened."

"I'll wait a day or two before going to see her," I said. "No reason for half the town to show up in the ER."

Colin pulled into a private driveway and turned around, then headed toward the outer road. He switched from concerned boss and friend to sheriff in nothing flat. "CSU couldn't get any good footprints in the stairwell because they'd been traveled over so much. I mean, there's plenty of prints in the dust, but not one clear print."

"Because the perp kept stepping over his own prints each time he used the stairwell?"

"Exactly," he said. "No prints on the panel, either."

"So what did you get?"

He gave me a questioning look.

"Well, you're obviously taking me somewhere," I said.

"When the wooden stairs get to the basement, they turn into concrete."

"Okay . . ."

"No prints on the concrete. And then the stairwell turns into a tunnel," he said. He put on his blinker and made a turn. He looked over at me again. "Put your seat belt on."

"Oh, sorry," I said. I did as he instructed. "You were saying something about a tunnel?"

"Yeah," he said. "The stairwell doesn't exit at the basement. In fact, there's no access to the basement at all from the stairwell. It leads down and then to a tunnel and then out of the city."

"What?" I said, stunned. "Did you say it leads out of the city?"

"Yes."

"Where does it come out?"

"It leads to an old cellar type of door on the other side of the creek. About six blocks from the Gaheimer House, just outside of town."

"Holy . . . but who the heck would build something that elaborate and why?"

"I don't know. I was hoping you could tell me."

"As far as I know none of this is on the surveys of the city or the blueprints of the Gaheimer House. I'll check again, though. Can we tell if it was built after the Gaheimer House was built, or was it part of the original construction?"

"I don't know," he said. "I just can't believe nobody in this town knew about this."

Colin parked on the side of the road just outside of town by the creek. He motioned for me to get out, and I followed him. We walked for at least ten minutes along the creek, swatting at mosquitoes and insects as we went. It was nearly dark, although still light enough that we could see where we were going. Crickets and cicadas played their symphony so loud that at one point it seemed like just one loud roar in my ears. The trees were black against the bruised curtain of dusk, and the creek *whished* swiftly off to my right.

A mosquito landed on my face and I smacked it. "I hate mosquitoes."

"I know," he said.

"If I get a tick on me, you're dead," I said. "Because you know, things that suck blood are just gross."

"We've had this discussion."

"I know."

"Hey, I coulda left you out of this," he said. "You'd be missing something pretty cool."

"All right, all right," I said.

Finally we came to an old dilapidated building that looked a lot like a fishing shack. Colin shined the flashlight on the ancient construction. One wall was caved in, leaning on the other three. Underneath that leaning wall was enough room for somebody to disappear beneath the cellar doors in the floor.

"I don't believe it," I said.

"You want to go down and take a look?"

"Are you serious?"

"Totally," he said.

"Okay," I said. He pulled open the cellar doors and descended some concrete steps. I followed. There were just enough stairs to make the tunnel about ten feet underground. Colin didn't need to duck his head, but he did so anyway. I think he didn't want anything dropping from the ceiling onto his hair. Who could blame him? A little way into the tunnel all light ceased to exist, save for the flashlight beam. The light seemed pretty thin and pretty weak, considering it was the only thing we had to keep us from bumping into walls that were barely eight feet apart and each other.

The musty odor was nearly enough to make me vomit. "There's enough mold down here to start my own penicillin lab."

"I thought they manufactured that synthetically nowadays," Colin said.

"Probably. What does that say about the twenty-first century? We have to synthetically grow fungus when it grows abundantly on its own."

I talked incessantly as long as Colin could stand it. I was far too nervous about being in a dark place with things that had hairy legs and fangs.

"Torie, relax."

"Right."

"They found some rodent bones," he said.

"Oh, joy."

We kept walking for what seemed like eternity, but I knew it wasn't. It doesn't take that long to walk six blocks. Then we came to the wooden stairs that led up into Wilma's old room. Colin stopped. "Right on that side of the wall is your basement."

"I can't believe this," I said.

"Pretty amazing, huh?"

"Yes."

"Well, I was wondering if you could help me with this inscription."

"Inscription?"

"Right here on the concrete wall."

> My *days be brighter*
> *Come the morn'*
> *Out of this shelter*
> My *life be born.*
>   P. B. 1862

"Possibly, but I'd have to check a few things first."

"Really? I should have known."

Twenty-Four

Half an hour later I was seated at my desk at the Gaheimer House wondering when and if I was ever going to get to go home. My head reeled with information, and it hurt because of all the gaps that I couldn't fill in.

Colin, Miller, and Newsome were walking through the Gaheimer House, talking on radios, taking measurements, and snapping pictures. Basically, I think they wanted me to feel that they were doing all they could to keep me safe. It was a sweet gesture if nothing else.

I only wished the world would stop for an hour. Just one hour.

The phone rang, and I answered it.

"Torie, what in blazes is going on?" Rudy asked.

"Long story," I said. "The so-called ghost that Stephanie and I have been hearing has been using an access panel in a closet wall, which leads out of the house through a tunnel to outside of town."

"Say what?"

"I know, surreal."

"Wait, did you know about this tunnel?"

"No."

"Who could have known about it?"

"I don't know."

"Well, at least we know you weren't hallucinating."

"I know."

Rudy was quiet a moment. "Look, about my mother—"

"Rudy, don't. We'll talk about it when I get home," I said. "I was a jerk."

"Y-you were?" he said. "I mean, you *were*. Really, Torie."

His tone was playful so I didn't go all ballistic. "We'll talk later."

"When later?"

"I don't know. I'm trying to help Colin figure out who could have known about the tunnel and who could have built it," I said. "I'll try not to be too late, but you may have to take the kids to school tomorrow."

"No biggie," he said.

We said our good-byes, and I stared at the phone for a moment after I placed it in its cradle. Taking a deep breath, I stretched and tried to mentally prepare myself for the long night ahead of me. I needed caffeine and sugar. In that order.

No sooner had I had thought it than Colin walked in and handed me a Dr Pepper and Chinese takeout. "I'm assuming you haven't eaten."

"No, I haven't," I said. I looked at the clock on my desk. It was after 8:00 P.M.

"So what do you think?"

"I think that sometime in the next hundred years the Blues will win the Stanley Cup."

"The tunnel. Come on."

"Let me ask you something first."

"What?" He took the containers of food out of the bag and placed them on my desk. Chinese food was something Colin and I did together. A little stepfather-stepdaughter activity, since my mother despised Chinese food and he never got to eat it otherwise.

It showed that he was at least working on thinking of me as something other than a pain in the butt.

"Do you think the same person who attacked Mike Walker attacked me?"

His hands hovered above the crab rangoon. "I think it's a very good possibility."

"Any reason why he would have attacked Mike?"

"I don't know. It's not like he witnessed the perp walking into the house. Now that we know how the perp was getting in, there's no way Mr. Walker could have known about it."

"You said Eleanore knew about Mr. Walker?"

"Yes," he said. "Are you suggesting Eleanore is the perp?"

"No. She's all bark, no bite. But she could have told somebody else in town."

"Like, maybe she told the wrong somebody?"

"Exactly."

"I'll ask her who she told," he said. "And I'll make it official business."

I took a bite of a vegetable egg roll. "Okay, here's what I think about the tunnel." I pulled a few pieces of paper out of a file and a book. "Hermann Gaheimer built this house in late 1861. He didn't actually move into it until about 1862. The exact date is sketchy, and so we've always just told the tourists that the house was built in the mid-1860s to be on the safe side. I am convinced that he built the stairwell and the tunnel when he built the house."

"Why?" Colin asked.

"Because, if you look at the house, there are no additions. Nothing's been changed. He had to have this space allocated from the get-go," I said. "I haven't been able to find original blueprints of the house or anything. I do have Hermann's diaries, which I read several years back. That's when I learned that he and Sylvia had had their torrid affair."

"She was about twenty and he was how old?" Colin asked and then shoved his mouth full of food.

"Old enough to be her grandfather," I said. "He never mentioned the tunnel or any clandestine activity that went on."

"Did you expect him to?"

"I don't know," I shrugged. "Maybe. At any rate, the house was built at the start of the Civil War. I know that Hermann Gaheimer was completely antislavery. He was a total abolitionist."

"Okay? So?"

"Colin, what do you know about the Underground Railroad?"

"Mmmm, that's how the slaves escaped to the North," he said.

"Yes," I said, "but they didn't actually ride on a railroad, and they didn't just walk to Canada or the northern states without help. The white people along the way, the safe houses, were the Underground Railroad. Many of these abolitionists lived in slave states, and they hid the slaves in cellars or compartments in the walls. You get where I'm going with this?"

"Ah, yes," he said. "You think Hermann was one of the contacts on the Underground Railroad?"

"Yes," I said. "It makes perfect sense. Even the poem carved in the wall of the tunnel. 'Out of this shelter . . . my life be born.' It's even dated 1862."

"Why the secrecy?"

"Well, contrary to what most people think, Missouri was a slave state."

"It was?"

"Yes. It was brought into the union as a slave state. The government added the state of Maine to the Union to bring balance back in."

"What do you mean?"

"Maine was not a slave state. The government didn't want one or the other to get the upper hand," I said. "It was called the Missouri Compromise."

"Oh, I remember that," he said.

"So the secrecy was because if anybody found out, Hermann's life would have been endangered. Antiabolitionist sentiments ran pretty high for a while, long after the emancipation. If Hermann ever told Sylvia, she probably chose not to tell anybody just because Sylvia was weird like that. She was always so secretive. But I don't think she knew."

"But still, if this is all true, what Hermann did was not only brave, it was very humanitarian. He should get some recognition for it."

"I have a feeling that Hermann wasn't about recognition, Colin. Here's his ledger," I said. "All through the years between 1862 and 1865 he has several entries for the amount of five dollars. Quite a bit of money back then. The only clue he gives as to who it went to was the letter S. I think this was the money he gave to the slaves to get the rest of the way out of the state."

"You just have his ledgers sitting around?" Colin asked with an incredulous look.

"No, they're on a shelf in Sylvia's old office. I grabbed them when I came up from the basement. Along with his diary. But there's no need for me to read that. I've already read it. It does make me want to read through all of his correspondence now."

Colin thought a moment. A contemplative silence filled the room. Finally, "Weren't the slaves freed before 1865, though?"

"Well, the Emancipation Proclamation was issued in the fall of 1862, but it didn't go into effect until January first of 1863. Even then, there was really no way for the government to enforce this proclamation. Basically, the slaves were freed as the Union took more territory. Some, obviously, weren't freed until the very end of the war. So throughout the war, there were slaves running to freedom."

"So now we know who built the tunnel and why."

"Yes. In fact, Hermann owned the land and the shack where the tunnel empties out. That was his fishing shack," I said and handed Colin a piece of paper showing the survey map.

"All right, so that mystery is solved. Now all we need to know is who, in the present day, figured out it was there and has been using it," Colin said.

"That's going to be a wee bit trickier," I said. "It could be any-body. It could be somebody from twenty miles away who happened upon it one day when he was hunting or fishing."

"True," he said. "But what would somebody like that have to gain from scaring you and your sister?"

"Nothing," I said. The hair stood up on my arms. I had forgot-ten this was personal. Suddenly I didn't want my Chinese food. I set my container down out of the way.

"Eat," he said. "You're losing weight."

"If I were trying to lose weight, people would say that with a lilt in their voices. 'Hey, girl, you're losing weight. Looking good.' But if I'm not trying it's like, 'Oh, you look awful. You need to eat.' Makes no sense."

"Your mother's worried."

"She's a mother."

"I guess you don't have a clue as to who is doing this?" he asked.

"Have you checked out Sylvia's family? They are the only ones who would stand to gain if something happened to me. They are the only people who might hold a grievance against me. Well, other than the mayor."

"I've spoken with them," Colin said. "Most of them couldn't care less. Only one of them, really, thought that they were entitled to something."

"Well, that's what they're saying, anyway. That doesn't mean that's how they really feel."

"True," Colin said. "I'll check out their alibis for the Strawberry Festival and today when Mr. Walker was attacked."

"And for all the times Steph or I reported a disturbance."

"Right," he said.

"There's just one thing that bothers me, Colin."

"Only one?"

"It's Sylvia. Sylvia heard noises, and we have reason to believe it was the perp who was standing at the foot of her bed one night," I said. "Somebody was stalking her before she died. That doesn't sound like a disgruntled heir. How could her family have known before she died that they weren't going to get anything? Would the whole thing even have occurred to them? And how would stalking her make her change her will?"

Colin stopped chewing.

"No, this is about something else, Colin. I feel it. I don't think this is about money at all."

"Unless there's somebody out there who wants revenge for something," he said.

"Exactly. But what? And why would I inherit the grudge, too?"

He put his chicken chow mein down on the desk. "I don't know," he said, "but I need to take you home and call it a night."

"Okay," I said. "Let me just grab some things. I can do some research from my home computer."

"Can you access the records here from home?" he asked.

"Some of them. At least, everything I need tonight."

Twenty-Five

When I finally arrived home it was well after nine and the kids were in bed already. I opened the door and took in the aroma of my house. Every house has a signature smell—whether it's a pleasant odor or not—and when I smelled my house I immediately began to relax. It was home. Refuge.

Fritz trotted up to me, and I reached down and scratched the back of his ears. He plopped over on his back and bared his belly to me. "You have no shame," I said to him.

"If I recall, I behave just like him when you scratch behind my ears," Rudy said from the doorway of the kitchen.

"Hi," I said. "Where's your mom?"

"She decided to spend the night at her sister's house."

"Oh," I said. "Sorry."

He shrugged.

"Look, Rudy," I said, "I'm really sorry about . . . everything. I've been behaving, well, repulsively, actually."

"I'm not totally blameless," he said.

"No, I know," I said. "You should have asked me if she could stay here. Regardless of what my answer would have been or how big the fight would have been, you should have asked."

"I know," he said.

"When my mother moved in, I specifically remember running it by you first."

"I know," he said. He shoved his hands into his pockets. "I know. I'm sorry."

"I've been such a jerk," I said. "I really need to speak to your mother."

"She'll be back in a few days. You didn't think you would scare her off, did you?"

"No," I said and laughed. I flopped down on the couch, and Rudy came over and sat next to me. He took my hand in his, and I leaned in and kissed him. "We can move if you want."

"Not on your life!" he said.

"Why?"

"Because you're not yourself right now. You're saying this based on the whole thing that happened with the historical society. If I took you up on it, within six months you'd want to come back," he said.

"So are you saying you would move if I wanted to?"

"No."

"Are you unhappy here?"

"No. This is my home," he said. He paused for a moment. "Well, I'm not saying I wouldn't like a new house. But I love New Kassel."

"Good," I said. "Let's not discuss it again."

"Fine with me," he said.

I laid my head on his shoulder and just sat there like that for the longest time. Finally I started getting sleepy and decided it was time to go to bed.

I slept like a baby for about three hours, and then something woke me up. I hate that feeling. It's almost like an invasion of my soul. I'm going along fine, sleeping, dreaming, doing that whole REM thing, and then, for no apparent reason at all, I'm awake, staring at the ceiling or the shadow puppets made by the tree branches outside my window.

When this happens, I usually strain my ears to pick up the faintest noises from downstairs. Is one of the kids up? Of course, I still have a baby monitor in the room for Matthew, so that helps to magnify whatever's going on down in the rest of the house. Tonight, there was nothing out of the ordinary. The usual soft whispers of Matthew's breathing and the occasional creak that most houses make were apparent. My mother always said, "The house is settling," any time there was an unexplained noise.

But there were no unexplained noises. In one of those unsolved mysteries of the human psyche, I was simply awake. Why would one deliberately wake up if one didn't have to?

I snuggled into Rudy's back and pulled the covers up to my chin.

Hermann Gaheimer had been a conductor on the Underground Railroad.

How cool was that? In all the excitement earlier in the day, I hadn't really had time to digest this news. This, of course, made me think of Sylvia. What would she have thought about this discovery? Of course, if Sylvia were alive I would never have discovered this, so there was no way, even in my greatest fantasy, that she could have found out. Still, I think she would be proud of him.

My mind raced with the idea. How many African slaves had he helped escape? I had found twelve entries in his ledgers where he'd given five dollars to S. But that didn't mean S was one person. It could have been a whole family each time. There was simply no way I would ever know. There was also the possibility that S didn't mean slave at all. Still, it was exciting just knowing that he'd been a part of the Underground Railroad, and that the Gaheimer House had such an honorable thing to add to its history. There was no mistaking the engraving on the wall.

Now I couldn't sleep. I'd gotten my mind thinking and working, and now I was wide awake. It wasn't fair.

I threw back the covers and went to my office adjacent to the bedroom. I booted up the computer and checked my mail. Laura James from the Iowa page had answered me.

> Torie,
> Thank you so much for the info. It's at least a lead that I can follow now. How's it going with the O'Shaughnessys?
> Laura

I jotted a response and went to Google to begin my search for Wayne Junction. Within half an hour I knew where the photograph of Millie O'Shaughnessy had been taken: on the corner of Wayne Junction and Germantown Avenue in Germantown, Pennsylvania. Germantown is no longer separate from Philadelphia, but at one time it was its own city. It was made part of Philadelphia sometime in the 1850s. I knew this because I actually had a few ancestors—Mennonites—from Germantown. They left in the early seventeen hundreds, though, so I'd had no reason to do any research on the modern-day city.

I rubbed my eyes and yawned. All right, now I knew where the photograph had been taken, but it didn't really get me any closer to knowing who the girl was or how Sylvia had known her or how she fit into Sylvia's life. And why the heck did I care?

I think you have forgotten your promise.

That was why.

Well, whatever the promise had been, I wasn't going to figure it out tonight. I went to the window and looked out at the river. The moon glinted off of the water like frosting on a deep blue cake. I reached for the phone and dialed Wisteria General Hospital. I asked for the ICU, and the nurse answered. It was after midnight, but there's always somebody awake in a hospital. "Yes, I was wondering if you could tell me how Mike Walker is doing?"

"Are you a member of the family?"

Why do they always ask that? It makes me think the worst. "No, I'm just a friend."

"He's doing pretty good," she said. "He's stabilized. He's in a lot of pain, but I think he's out of the woods."

"That's good," I said. "When can he have visitors?"

"As long as it's only for a few minutes, you can come tomorrow," the nurse said.

"Thanks," I said.

I hung up the phone and went back to staring out at the river. I needed to pop in a movie—a boring one—and try to fall asleep. But watching the water was hypnotic, too, and if I stared at it long enough I would fall asleep standing right there. I love big bodies of water. They are so soothing. I have never lived in a place that is landlocked. No water for fifty miles in any direction—I can't imagine what that's like. If for no other reason, the Mississippi is great because it always gives you a sense of direction. If you're headed toward the river, you're headed east, at least in Granite County. But I love the sound of the water more than anything, and since the only things separating my house and the river were my yard, River Pointe Road, and the railroad tracks, I was close enough to hear it.

Just then I saw a silhouette walking along the river. It was human, as opposed to animal. The person was walking head down, hands shoved deep in his pockets. Then, almost as if he knew I was watching, he stopped and turned right toward my house. A full minute must have passed as the silhouette stared up at my house. Just standing there.

I shivered all the way to my toes. "Rudy!" I ran to the bed. "Rudy, wake up."

"I don't care where the dog pooped, I'm fishing."

"Rudy!" I said and shook him.

"What?" he screeched. "What? What?"

"There's somebody outside."

In the moonlight I could see the confusion on his face. His eyes crossed and he rubbed them. "Are you telling me you woke me up to tell me somebody is outside?"

"Yes."

"He's outside, we're inside. What's the problem?"

"Rudy, come and look!" I tugged on his arm.

He scratched his armpit and yawned. "You know, I only married you because I want to be beatified when I die."

"Great, come here!" I said, still tugging on his arm.

He made his way around the pile of dirty clothes, managed to step on Fritz—who went scurrying under the bed—and stumbled over a pile of books. When his toe hit a box, he'd had his fill. "Dammit, Torie! If you want me to walk in the dark, you better make sure the path is clear! Oh, my toe!"

"Sorry," I said.

"This better be good."

"Right there," I said and hid behind the curtains. "Out there by the river."

Rudy said nothing as he looked out.

"Do you see him?"

"Torie," he said, "it's one of the homeless. You know, they walk the railroad tracks all the time."

"No, no," I said. "They don't usually stare at you through the window and look menacing."

"Maybe he's wishing he had this house. You know, maybe he's thinking back to his former life."

I smacked myself in the head. "Ugh. He was staring right at me."

"Well, when I saw him, he turned and walked away. He's proba- bly just dreaming of life in a real house," Rudy said. "I can't believe you actually woke me up for this." He walked back to our bedroom and hit the same box with his toe on the way back. This time he let out a string of expletives a mile long. My name was attached to a few of them.

I looked back out the window and the person was gone.

Just as I turned to go I saw him standing under the tree in our front yard.

"Rudy!"

"Oh, for God's sake, woman!"

"He's in our front yard, under the tree!"

"Call 911," he said. "Don't turn on the lights."

"Where are you going?" I asked.

"Down to be with the kids."

"All right."

I didn't dial 911. When you're the stepdaughter of the sheriff, you call the source directly. It's faster. The switchboard secretary answered. "Peg, it's Torie. Get somebody out here, now!"

"What's the problem, Torie?" Peg asked.

"Prowler. He's on our property. With what's been going on at the Gaheimer House, this can't be a coincidence."

"Gotcha. Colin's on his way out the door."

I slammed the phone down and ran down the steps. "Rudy?"

"In here," he said.

I hit the bottom step into the kitchen, rounded the corner, and ran down the hallway to where he stood. I was out of breath and slightly hysterical. My breath came in ragged gasps.

"Calm down," he said. "Shh. Let's not wake the kids if we don't have to."

Just then I heard glass shatter. I screamed, and Rudy clamped his hand over my mouth. "Get Matthew. I'll get the girls."

Another window broke somewhere in the house. The glass shrieked as it was hit and then crashed to the ground. I grabbed Matthew out of his bed in the dark and met Rudy back in the hall-way.

"Daddy? What's wrong?" Rachel asked. Another window broke and she screamed. "Oh, my God!"

"What's happening?" Mary cried.

"To the garage, everybody."

Rudy was smart. There were no windows in the garage. What's more, we could get to it without leaving the house, then drive away. Rudy and I managed to herd the kids and ourselves into the garage. Then he turned and locked the door behind him. "Get in the car!"

We tried to do as he instructed, but the girls were sobbing and Matthew was now wide awake. Matthew reached for Rachel and she took him, trying to be the brave big sister. Once my arms were free, Mary grabbed my legs. "Honey, get in the car," I said. My hands shook and my voice cracked. I tried to stay strong for my children, but deep down I just wanted to cry and run. I'd like to think that if Rudy hadn't been there I would have been smart enough to think of the garage, but I'm not sure I would have.

"Sit with me!" Mary cried.

I got in the backseat with her and placed her on my lap. Rachel hugged Matthew close. I didn't know my heart could beat this fast or this hard. "Rudy, did you get the keys?"

"I grabbed them off the shelf as we came by."

Rudy sat perfectly still for a moment.

"What's the matter?" I said from the backseat.

"If I open this door and he's standing there . . ."

"No, Daddy! Don't open the door," Rachel cried. "Just wait for Grandpa to come."

"Maybe she's right, Rudy," I said. "Colin's on his way. Besides, the guy has made so much noise, he's probably taken off by now. Let's just wait and see."

Rudy's shoulders relaxed a bit, and he sat back against the seat. "Okay, everybody just calm down," he said. "Let's be quiet and listen."

The children couldn't be quiet. They were far too scared. "All right," I said. "Let's sing a song."

"Oh, right, Mom," Rachel said.

I flicked her ear. "Let's sing," I said. "How about one of those songs you guys learned at camp last year? Something about a baby kangaroo. That's my favorite. Come on, how does it go?"

Mary started singing, and then Rachel, reluctantly and through sobs and snot, joined in. There we sat in the dark garage singing some stupid song about a pink kangaroo, tears running down our faces, our house being violated, until there was a bang on the garage door.

My heart stopped and I clutched at Mary. The girls both squealed.

"Shhh, everybody shut up," Rudy said.

We all did our best to be quiet when we heard the bang again—and then a muffled voice. "Rudy? Torie? It's Colin!"

"Oh, thank God," Rachel said.

"Grandpa Badge!" Mary cried out.

Rudy hit the button on the garage door opener, and as the door raised I could see Colin's feet, then his torso, and finally his face, looking mean and pissed off. His hand rested on the butt of his gun. I can honestly say that I have never been so happy to see any human being in all of my life. I laid my head back and swallowed.

Then I lost it. Sobs broke free, and I cried into Mary's back.

Twenty-Six

We spent the night at Colin and my mother's house. When we awoke the next morning—after a fitful night's sleep— Colin had four rocks sitting on his kitchen table. Four big rocks in plastic evidence bags. Next to them were four pieces of paper and a dozen or so rubber bands in plastic evidence bags. The pieces of paper all simply read, "Move, or be moved."

I have never been so cold. It was a coldness that began in my stomach and feathered out to the tips of my fingers and toes. Even my heart was cold. As a result, I felt as if my blood were slugging along in my veins, not really in any hurry to get to its destination.

"What does this mean?" my mother said. Her eyes were wide with fear, and her chin trembled slightly when she spoke.

"I think, Mom, somebody is trying to get me out of town."

"First they attack you at the Strawberry Festival," Rudy said.

"Then the historical society vote," Colin said.

"The attempts at making you afraid in the Gaheimer House," Rudy said.

"Mike Walker," Colin added.

"And now my family," I finished.

"Whoever it is, they're a ball of contradictions," Rudy said.

"What do you mean?" I asked and hugged myself.

"Well, on one hand, they're gutsy enough to attack a family that is widely loved and supported *and* related to the sheriff. Me," Colin said. "Shows a complete lack of respect for authority. On the other hand, they didn't kill you or Mike Walker, so they're not gutsy enough to commit murder."

"Thank goodness," my mother said.

"Their behavior also goes a long way to prove that they want everything left intact when you go," Colin said.

"What do you mean?"

"I mean they're banking on you either selling the Gaheimer House or giving it to somebody, along with everything in it. You walk off and leave the officer's chairs wide open, as well. In other words, whoever is after what Sylvia left you would be free to try to obtain it," Colin said.

"Isn't that sort of short-sighted?" I asked. "Won't we be able to figure out that whoever buys the Gaheimer House would be the one who did all of this?"

"Maybe not. Maybe they're working with somebody else. Maybe they've got a puppet to install. Or maybe it's not about their getting the Gaheimer House and historical society. Maybe it's just all about you not getting it," Colin said. "Whichever, we've got definitive proof now of what their ultimate goal is. Getting you to move."

"Does the perp think this will work?" I said.

My mother handed me a glass of Dr Pepper and one of her world-famous apricot bars. Comfort food. She's so good. I took a bite and, believe it or not, my stomach lurched and it nearly didn't go down.

"I don't know," Colin said.

"I mean, everybody knows now that somebody is trying to run me out of town."

"It could be they thought you would react differently to the whole historical society thing," he said.

"Meaning?"

"Meaning they didn't expect you to take your toys and go home. They didn't expect you to take the Gaheimer House and tell them to found their own historical society. If you lost the vote, they expected you to hand everything over quietly. And just because you won the vote doesn't mean that you wouldn't have been removed from office by some later scandal," Colin said.

"Like something they planned?"

"Oh, I've no doubt. But when you told them to go get their own toys, they panicked. And thus they had to kick up the threat," he said and pointed to the rocks on the table. "I'm not so sure it was ever meant to go this far."

"It's like high school," I said.

"Yeah, well, some people's mental age never gets beyond fourteen."

"Oh, that's comforting," I said.

"At any rate, you guys should stay here until we figure out who's behind this," he said. "I can't even imagine they'd try anything here."

"What about the Gaheimer House?" I asked.

The phone rang, and my mother answered it.

"What about it?" Colin asked.

"Is it safe to go there?"

"Why?" he asked.

"Torie, I don't know—" Rudy said.

"Because I think the answer to this might be in some of the records we have," I said.

"What do you mean?"

"Obviously, whoever is doing this thinks they were entitled to what I got," I said. "Maybe I can find a record of it. I should probably go to the courthouse as well and see if Sylvia was ever sued by anybody."

"Good point," Colin said.

"You're supposed to be on my side," Rudy said to Colin.

"She's right, though. If Sylvia was ever sued, that could be a big lead. It's obvious Sylvia was worried that somebody would try something once she was gone, or she wouldn't have been so nervous about her will being contested," Colin said.

"True," I said.

Mom hung up the phone and turned back to the conversation. "It was Stephanie," she said. "She wanted to know if she should come in to work today. She couldn't reach you at your house or your cell phone, so she thought to try here. I just filled her in on everything that happened."

"Oh, what if the person had thrown rocks into the Gaheimer House when Stephanie was there?" I said. "She's pregnant. She could have been hurt."

"Whoever it is doesn't want the Gaheimer House hurt," Colin said.

"So it would seem," I said. "Mom, what did you tell Steph?"

"I told her not to come in until you had spoken with her," she said.

"Good. I'm going to the courthouse," I said.

"I'll go with you," Rudy said.

"The kids can stay with me," Mom said. "I think they should stay home from school today, anyway."

"All right," I said. Suddenly, a thought struck me. "Oh, and while we're here, I want to go by Wisteria General and see Leigh Duran."

"Right," Rudy said.

"Oh, jeez."

"What?" Rudy asked.

"Tomorrow is Saturday. The second weekend in the Strawberry Festival. I have so much to do."

"I'll have Tobias call everybody and make sure everything is ready to go," Colin said. "He can be in charge for a day."

"All right," I said. "I'm off to the courthouse."

"Eat your apricot bar," Mom said. "You're losing weight."

Twenty-Seven

Believe it or not, there were some records I did not have at the Gaheimer House, namely, all of the civil court records and the more recent marriage and probate records. Rudy and I pulled into the parking lot of the courthouse in Wisteria, and I glanced around nervously. It was difficult for me to drive around and not wonder if somebody was watching from the shadows. "Thanks for coming along," I said.

"Hey, you went fishing with me in Minnesota. This is the least I could do."

"That's right, I did," I said. "Well, this is a lot more fun than fishing."

He rolled his eyes.

Two hours later he was rubbing his eyes. And sneezing. "I cannot believe you'd rather be in here with all of these musty old books than out on a lake or a riverbank."

"Oh, if I could find court records out on a lake, I'd be in heaven. But they don't have filing cabinets on lakes."

"Find anything?" he asked.

"Nothing so far," I said.

"Well, I think I did," he said and pulled out a book. *"Pershing vs. Burgermeister."*

"What?"

"Looks like Sylvia had a restraining order against Virgie and Harold Burgermeister back in the sixties."

"Oh, let's request the original on this," I said. We put in our request for the original file with a file clerk named Bernadine Shankmeyer, who not only knew me by name but asked how my sister was doing. Rudy just shook his head. I kept looking through the indexes. By the time the original came back on the restraining order, I had found two other records that I wanted to look at.

"What does it say?" Rudy asked.

"Basically, it reads that Harold and Virgie were not allowed within two hundred feet of Sylvia—hard to manage considering they lived in a small town. Anyway, looks like Harold had physically attacked Sylvia at a picnic. Oh, this is interesting. Make a note for me to go by and talk to Virgie and Harold."

I pulled out my cell phone and called Colin. "Brooke," he said.

"Colin, it's Torie. I found a record for a restraining order Sylvia had against the Burgermeisters."

"Charity?"

"No, her in-laws. Harold and Virgie. What have you found?"

"Well, I talked to Eleanore," he said. "She said she only told one person about there being a private detective at the Gaheimer House."

"Who did she tell?"

"Danny Eisenbach."

"Colin, he was one of the people who showed some discontent with my leadership at the meeting the other night."

"Well, I'm pulling into his driveway now. But remember, he could have told ten people by this time. It doesn't mean he's our man."

"I know. Anything else?"

"Yeah," he said. "I asked her why she had taken the stand against you at the meeting."

"And her answer was?"

"That a group of townspeople had been talking at the last box social and the subject of you came up, and she said before you knew it, there was a consensus that you should be removed from power."

"Gee, wonder what would happen if I ran for mayor?"

"Oh, don't even go there," he said. "Besides, I'm running."

"What? Get out of here."

"No, really, I've decided I'm running against Bill next term."

"But . . . can you be sheriff and mayor at the same time?"

Rudy shot me a look with his eyebrows raised.

"No," Colin said.

"But . . . you can't seriously not be sheriff."

"We'll talk about it later," he said.

"Did Eleanore happen to say who all was at this box social?"

"I don't know," he said, "but it was at the Methodist church, so I guess you could just see who attends the church and narrow it down from there. More than likely, you're looking at one or two people doing the talking and everybody else falling into place."

"Well, it's possible there were people in attendance that aren't necessarily members of the church, too."

"Right."

"How'd it go on the alibis of Sylvia's family?"

"Everybody's checking out except David, but even he had an alibi for most of the times in question," he said. "Charlie was out of town all week. The Franklins, both Julie and Steve, were at some sort of retreat the day of the Strawberry Festival. Toni was at work. And then, oh, who's the other sister?"

I scanned my mind. He'd mentioned David and Charlie. He'd mentioned Julie and Toni. That left . . . oh, who was the other grand niece of Sylvia's? "Susan!"

"That's right. Susan was at a competition."

"A what?"

"She's a champion horse rider. English style."

"Oh." Learn something new every day. "All right," I said. "I'll get back to you if I find anything else."

"Hey, Torie. Elmer goes to the Methodist church," he said. "Why don't you call him and see if he remembers anything funny going on at the last box social. If he even attended."

"I will," I said. I felt uneasy suddenly. *Maybe they've got a puppet.* What if Elmer was the one wanting me out of office and he was just pretending to be on my side? The mastermind behind the whole thing could be pretending to support me all along and be pushing somebody else's buttons.

"What's the matter?" Rudy asked.

"Nothing," I said. "I'm just getting paranoid."

Rudy grabbed my hand and squeezed it. "Don't," he said. "Plenty of people love you in this town."

"But it only takes one crazy one to bring it all down."

"You'll be fine. Crazy people never win."

"I just can't believe this is happening."

"Whoever it is is seriously messed up in the head," he said. "People who would actually act out against somebody because they were jealous . . . well, they're just not whole people. There's something missing in them. Unless they're like sixteen, because teenagers are just weird."

"What's missing in them?"

"A soul, for one thing," he said. "They're not complete."

"All right," I said and sighed. "I want to see these other two records, and then I'm heading back to the Gaheimer House. I want to make sure everything is all right."

"You heard Colin," he said. "Whoever it is doesn't want to harm the Gaheimer House."

"I don't care," I said. "I still want to check it."

"All right."

"But I want to run by the hospital first. Oh, and then the Methodist church," I said.

"Why?"

"I want to see Leigh."

"No, the church," he said.

"I want a list of their members. You know, I have never paid attention to who goes to what church. I just realized I can't begin to tell you what religion anybody is in our town."

"Does it matter?"

"Today it does."

•

I hate the smell of hospitals, but I think it's psychological. My daughter Mary loves the smell of hospitals. She wants to be a doctor. I told her that she might wait and make up her mind based on, well, if she can pass biology, rather than based on the fact she likes the smell of hospitals. Have I mentioned that she's weird?

Rudy and I stopped outside of Leigh Duran's hospital room. I took a deep breath first and then knocked. I heard the nurse say to come in. We walked in to find Leigh surrounded by a sea of flowers. The room smelled like roses and hyacinths. I said hello to the nurse, who left quietly. I realized the reason I was so apprehensive about seeing Leigh was that I wasn't sure what sort of condition she would be in. That, and I felt sorry for her. I wasn't sure if sympathy would be a good thing to show or not. It might make her feel worse, or it could be the very thing she needed to see from people. I didn't know.

She lay on the bed with her nondescript brown hair plastered on her head and trailing on the pillow. She was pale, her eyes sunken and bruised looking. Then I noticed the white bandages around her wrists. I glanced for a second and then vowed I would only look at her eyes for the rest of the visit.

Leigh is not what I'd call a good friend, but like a lot of people in town, I did know her. She was married to Edwin Duran, and with Colin being my stepfather that meant they were in our social circle more often than not. I suppose my real problem was I wasn't sure I knew her well enough to have a pool of useless chatter to pull from, and awkward silences right now were not what I wanted.

"Leigh," I said. Should I ask how she was feeling?

"Torie, Rudy," she said. She tried to straighten herself in the bed. Then she ran a very shaky hand through her lank hair.

"How are you feeling?" Rudy asked.

"Oh, I'm doing all right," she said. But her eyes said otherwise. Her eyes spoke volumes in pain and despair.

"Edwin just went down to grab a bite to eat," she said.

"Oh," I said. "Well, we can't stay long, so if we miss him, tell him we said hello."

"I will," she said.

"So," I said and sighed. "I think my husband is going to make a pig of himself again this weekend."

"More pie contests for you?" she asked.

Rudy rubbed his belly. "Can't help myself."

She smiled, but only just.

We talked a little more about the Strawberry Festival. I tried not to mention children in any way, because I didn't want to upset her. So I made a few jokes about my mother winning a year's supply of bagels. In fact, I think Rudy and I sort of overdid it on the bagel jokes, and suddenly there was an awkward silence. That very thing I wanted to avoid.

Leigh's gaze flicked around the room, landing on everything except my face. She turned to Rudy then. "Do you really think that if you commit suicide you don't go to heaven?"

"Oh, Leigh, don't ask me that," he said, looking for all the world as though he'd just swallowed a frog.

"No, I want to know what you think. Because I thought God would be happy with people who wanted to go home bad enough to take their own lives."

"I think the point is that only God has the right to give or take life," Rudy said. "But what do I know, Leigh? I'm just a plumbing salesman."

"That's what Edwin said," she said and picked at her bandages, which I'd vowed only moments ago not to look at.

"What, that he's a plumbing salesman?" Rudy asked.

"No, that I wouldn't go to heaven."

"I . . ." Rudy said.

I was a little peeved at Duran for telling her such a thing. The woman was obviously unstable; why would he tell her something like that? I reached out to touch her arm, but something in her body language made me stop just short of touching her. I'm not so sure I'd want people touching me, either, if I were in her state.

"You know, it's not that I hate it here or anything," she said. "I just don't see the point."

Time was up. I couldn't do this one second longer. We said good-bye and wished her well. At the elevator, Rudy pushed the button. Neither one of us said a word for the longest time. Finally, Rudy said, "Why did we come to visit her, again?"

"Rudy."

"That was God-awful, Torie. Absolutely horrible."

"With my position in town, and especially with our new inheritance—not to mention we're her landlords—it's sort of expected of us."

"Are you serious?"

"It comes with the territory, Rudy. Get used to it."

•

Rudy pulled the car in at the Methodist church, which is actually almost to Meyersville and not in New Kassel at all. But there isn't a Methodist church in New Kassel, so anybody who lives in New Kassel who's a Methodist would attend church here.

The day was warm, probably at least ninety degrees—a little too warm for my taste—and the sky was a brilliant deep blue. The church was stark white, and it hurt my eyes to look at it for long against the bold azure. I was grateful for the display Mother Nature was giving, because what I'd seen in the hospital was too depressing for words. I walked into a door on one side of the building that said OFFICE and found Nathan Tate sitting behind the desk. I went to school with Nathan years ago. I didn't want to think about or admit just how many years ago it had been. He had moved to Meyersville right after high school, so I only saw him at special events and in the occasional restaurant.

"Nathan," I said. "Nice to see you."

"Well, hello, Torie," he said.

"You remember Rudy?"

"Yes," he said and held out his hand, which my husband shook. "We've met a few times. What can I do for you? I thought our cemetery had already been recorded by the historical society."

"Oh, it has," I said. "I'm actually here to get a copy of your directory."

"You thinking about joining?" he said and moved around his desk to a box that sat on the floor.

"No," I said. "I'm compiling a list of the churches in the area, thought it would be good to have a directory from each one. You never know when that information might be needed."

"Well, I don't have this year's back from the printers," he said. He handed me a small booklet of maybe ten pages printed on front and back. "So last year's will have to do."

"Not a problem," I said.

"I can tell you the Assembly of God church out on Highway P doesn't make a directory," he said.

"Oh, no?"

"No," he said. "I asked them who their printer was when I was thinking about doing this one, and they said they didn't print a directory."

"Oh," I said, simply because I wasn't sure what else I was supposed to say.

"How are the kids?" he asked.

"Doing great."

"I heard you had another one. Is this four?"

"No, three," I said. "He's actually almost two now."

"Wow, time flies."

"I know."

There was a silence between all of us, the kind of silence that follows when people who really have nothing to say to each other finally run out of small talk. "Well, I'll see you, Nathan."

"Sure, come by any time," he said.

As we walked out of the church office, Rudy shot me a look that I wasn't sure I could decipher. "What?"

"You lie really good," he said.

"I know."

"It's scary."

"Well, I don't lie to you."

"Never?"

"I'm not saying never," I said. "But if I do, it's only to keep you safe."

"Ha!"

We got in the car, and I started thumbing through the directory.

"That poor guy," Rudy said.

"Who?"

"Mr. Tate in there. Nathan Tate. Do you realize his nickname would have been—"

"Nate Tate. I know," I said. "I went to school with him. Remember?"

"Parents can be cruel."

"So can playground children."

"So, where to next?"

"The Gaheimer House," I said.

"Are you going to eat anytime soon? I'm hungry."

"Why don't you drop me off at my office and then you go get us something to eat?"

"From where?" he asked.

"Surprise me."

"Oh, last time I did that, you wouldn't speak to me for days."

I just smiled at him.

•

I stepped into the Gaheimer House and took a deep breath. Afternoon sun glistened off the marble floor I knew so well—the marble floor that Sylvia and I had walked across a thousand and one times giving tours. I loved the marble floors in the sitting room. They were so much easier to clean than the hardwood floors throughout the rest of the house. Speaking of cleaning, the house needed to be cleaned.

As I walked through the room, I straightened a lace doily on the back of the divan. I had seen Sylvia do that exact same thing at least twice a day, whether it was crooked or not. Now I had begun the tradition. The doily hadn't needed straightening. It was just something I felt I needed to do.

"What have you done to me, Sylvia?" I asked the air. Which did not respond, by the way. I considered that a good thing.

I went to the kitchen first and looked at the boxes on the table. I carried three of them out to the back porch for the Vincentians to pick up. There were two left. The phone rang, and I jumped. "This is Torie," I said.

"Hey, Miller's coming over to house-sit with you," Colin's voice said.

"Why?"

"Well, just to be on the safe side. In case somebody comes back through that tunnel. Especially after last night. We've placed a guy at the entrance by the creek, but still, just in case the perp would slip by," he said.

"All right," I said.

"I woulda sent Duran. He's been hurting for cash lately . . . but . . ."

"Yeah, I know," I said, remembering Leigh's pale face and sunken eyes.

"So, anyway, Miller won't be in uniform. This is on my dime."

"Colin—"

"It's not in the budget, but I really feel you should have somebody there."

"I'll be watching for him, then."

I carried a box into my office and then went back and got the other one, because there was no way I could carry two boxes at once. Even if I hadn't still been a little sore from last Saturday, my arms weren't long enough to wrap around two boxes. Short people are at a distinct disadvantage in this world.

The phone rang again, and I answered it. "Torie," I said.

"Hello, it's Tobias Thorley."

"Oh, Tobias, what can I do for you?"

"Do you have the list of bands for this weekend?"

"Yes, I do. As a matter of fact, one of them is supposed to come by today and see what the stage looks like."

"Do you mind if I come get the list?"

"No, come on by," I said.

"See you in a bit," he said.

I pulled a pile of papers out of one of the boxes and sat down to begin deciphering what was what. I have no idea why sitting at my desk and going through piles of old papers comforts me, but it does. I didn't want to just come by and "check on things" like I'd told Rudy. I wanted to be surrounded by the familiar. That can be a stronger drug than any medicine.

I booted up the computer, and the phone rang again. "This is Torie."

"Torie, it's Stephanie," she said. "Do you need help with the Strawberry Festival this weekend? Because if you don't, I think we're going to go shopping for the baby. Especially since all I have are girl things and this one is a boy."

"No, sure, you go ahead and go shopping."

"Well, I don't need to go both days. Which one do you think you'd need me the most for?"

"No, Steph, you've done a lot. If you want to come down over the weekend, you pick the day."

"All right," she said. "I'll probably see you Sunday."

"Good," I said.

"Are you guys all right?" Her voice turned serious.

"I've been better," I said. Then I sighed. "I was really scared, Steph. I don't think I've ever been that scared. It's one thing when I'm in danger, but it's a whole different ball game when it's my family."

"I can't even imagine."

My hands started to shake just thinking about it.

"Well, I hate to hit you with anything else," she said.

"What?"

"Have you seen the *Post* today?"

"Honey, I haven't seen a paper in a week."

"Rossini's article made it."

"Whose article?" I stopped. "Oh, the one about me?"

"Yup," she said. "I'll save it for you if you can't get one."

"Do I want to read this article?"

"I don't know."

"If it were about you, would you be happy?"

She was quiet on the other end.

"Say no more," I said. There was a knock on the door. "Steph, I've gotta go. Somebody's here."

"Okay, I'll see you Sunday."

I answered the door, half expecting it to be Rudy, but instead it was Deputy Miller. "Hey, Deputy, come on in."

He took off his hat and said, "Mrs. O'Shea."

"Make yourself comfortable. I mean, I don't think you have to stand on guard. Believe it or not, there's a television in the kitchen if you want to watch it. There might even be something in the fridge."

"All right," he said. "That television doesn't get cable, does it?"

"No," I said and smiled. I headed back to my office, and he went to the kitchen and turned on the television. I thumbed through more of Sylvia's personal papers. Some of them were from as far back as 1918. I don't think she ever threw anything away. One letter in particular caught my attention. The return address was Philadelphia, Pennsylvania. With trembling fingers I pulled the single-page handwritten letter from the yellowed envelope. It read:

13th August 1928

Miss Sylvia Pershing,

With genuine respect, I write to you on this day to inquire whether or not you intend to honor your previous agreement with Mrs. O'Shaughnessy. Write to me straightaway or I shall make other arrangements.

With sincerity,
Father Riley Kincaid

To say the least, I was stunned. Mrs. O'Shaughnessy had to be none other than Millie's mother. Well, I suppose she could have been her grandmother. The year on the letter would be about when the photograph of Millie had been taken at the Wayne Junction sign. In fact, I could probably safely assume that the photograph arrived in this letter. Somehow I got the feeling that this wasn't the first letter they sent to Sylvia. It certainly wasn't the last, because sometime later a postcard arrived reminding her of her promise.

I pulled the postcard out of my purse—I still carried it with me everywhere—and flipped it over. The handwriting was the same. Father Riley Kincaid had sent this postcard to Sylvia.

"You've got mail," my computer said.

I had quite a bit of mail, actually, but ignored the things that would require me to sit down and write in response for half an hour. I clicked on the mail from Laura James.

Torie,

I have a lead for you. I have been doing some research for two members of our historical society. Their parents had been orphan train riders, and this is somewhat my area of expertise. In so doing, I have been scouring the orphanage records. Guess whose name I found at the Sisters of Notre Dame House of Mercy in Dubuque? You betcha. Millie O'Shaughnessy. She was there from 1929 to late 1933. The records only state that her mother's name was Lucille, that she was Catholic, and that she was born in New York City in 1924. The really bad news is, she was never adopted. She ran away. She disappeared into the streets like so many others. In fact, in the 1850s it was estimated that some 30,000 children were living on the streets of New York, without parents or shelter. The numbers of homeless children were at epidemic highs later, after the influx of immigrants at the turn of the century. On one hand, I suppose this helps you. On the other—since she disappeared— I can't imagine that this comes as good

news. Let me know if you need anything else. If she indeed arrived on an orphan train (the Catholic orphan trains were called "mercy trains," by the way), I might be able to help you with more complete records.
Sincerely,
Laura James

If I thought I was stunned before, now my mouth was literally gaping open. I dashed off a quick response to Laura thanking her and telling her that she succeeded in causing quite a jaw-dropping experience for me. Then I told her that anything else she could provide would be helpful but that I didn't know whether Millie was on the "mercy trains" or not. I did have reason to believe she had been, at one time, under the care of one Father Riley Kincaid.

Who was Millie O'Shaughnessy? How did she know Sylvia? Could it be that Sylvia had promised to take Millie in? But if she had, how had she known Millie's mother, who lived in New York? Sylvia never seemed like the type to even consider taking a child in. She could barely tolerate children. Based on what I knew of Sylvia, the notion of her taking Millie to raise seemed utterly preposterous.

Of course, I had to remind myself that Sylvia was an iceberg. I only knew the last thirty years of Sylvia's life, the years on the surface. Another seventy years lay beneath the water.

There was a knock on the door, and Miller ran by my office. "I'll get it."

A few moments later, Rudy walked into my office with turkey sandwiches from the Smells Good Cafe. "Oh, that smells really good," I said.

"Thus the name. I bought extras," he said. "Let me give one to Miller."

He went to give the deputy his sandwich, and I continued staring at Father Kincaid's letter. Rudy came back in and emptied the bag, producing three extra sandwiches. He shrugged. "You never know who might come by," he said.

More likely he'd have tons of leftovers for a late-night snack, but I didn't vocalize my opinion because he seemed so proud of himself. There was another knock on the door, which Miller ran to answer, and a few moments later Helen Wickland walked in. "Hey, Torie. Rudy."

I stood. "What can I help you with?" I said.

She had a newspaper clutched in her hands. "I came by for two reasons. One was to apologize for the other night," she said. "I'm not sure what exactly it is I'm apologizing for, other than I wasn't very vocal in sticking up for you. But I won't apologize for running against you. When Eleanore nominated me, I didn't even think about you getting upset. We're grown adults. I just thought it would be fun to be an officer in the historical society."

"I'm not upset with you for running against me, Helen. That would be silly of me," I said. "I was upset because I was being attacked, and I suppose I expected a more valiant effort from more people in the room. Don't worry about it. It was an eye-opener for me."

"I thought you might want to see the paper," she said.

"Oh," I said and took the paper from her. Then the phone rang. I answered it. "Hello?"

"Jesus H. Christ, have you seen the freaking paper?" It was Collette. My best friend.

"I just had it handed to me."

"Why didn't you tell me Rossini interviewed you? I could have watched for this article and, I dunno, maybe done something about it before it went to press," she said.

"I haven't read it yet, so . . . I meant to tell you. Actually, I meant to ask you about this Rossini guy, but so much has happened I just haven't gotten around to it. Jeez," I said. "In fact, I had forgotten all about the damn interview."

"Did you really tell this guy that Sylvia clawed her way to the top—making New Kassel the thriving tourist attraction that it is— by not allowing pond scum to own their own homes?"

"What? No!"

"I'm going to tear this guy in two," Collette said. "He'll never work in this town again. Damn columnist. He thinks he can get by with anything by not quoting you."

"Huh?"

"Oh, if it's Rossini's interpretation or opinion of you, he thinks he can say whatever he wants. Jerkwad thinks he's damn Rush Limbaugh."

"Calm down."

"Calm down?" Collette said. "Torie, did you say that you thought it was your appointment from God to carry on Sylvia's work and to keep the rednecks from taking over your little Kingdom of New Bavaria?"

"What?!" I sat down. "Oh, he did not print that. Did he really print that?"

Rudy had stopped chewing his sandwich, and Helen was shaking her head and blushing all the way to her ears. I could only imagine what I must have looked like. There probably wasn't an inch on me that wasn't red from anger or flushed with hives. "I did not say either of those things."

"Sue his ass for libel, girl," Collette said.

"Collette, I have to go. I'll call you back later."

I hung up the phone and went about reading the article that Helen had brought to me. It was one slanderous comment after another. He even described me as a "short and dumpy soccer mom who is cashing in on the timely death of her associate."

I stood up. "How in the hell can he print this?"

Then I sat down.

Then I stood up.

Watching me get up and down, Rudy looked like one of those bobblehead toys. "Sugar, sweetie, pick one, up or down. You're making me seasick."

The phone rang.

"Hello?"

"Well, well, well," Mayor Castlereagh said. "We finally see the true colors of our Little Miss Historian."

"Oh, I bet you're loving this," I said.

"You know I am," he said. "Those chickens will be gone by sundown."

"Listen here, you . . . you . . . If you touch one feather on my chickens . . ."

"Yes?"

I slammed the receiver down into the cradle.

"Bill?" Rudy said.

"Yeah."

"Torie, what are you going to do?" Helen said.

"Look, Collette can pull strings and get this retracted," I said. "I'll . . . I'll write a formal apology to the town of New Kassel in our *Gazette*. Everything will be fine."

Deep down inside, though, I couldn't help but wonder whether it *would* all be fine. Once the suspicion was planted, people would always wonder. But I couldn't think about that now. Somebody seriously wanted my reputation ruined, wanted me gone, out of power, and out of town, even.

I looked down at the list of members that I'd gotten from the Methodist church. I knew tons of people on that list. Hell, even Deputy Duran and my mother were on it. Not that my mother ever went to church, but that was the church she belonged to. But two names popped out at me. Eleanore Murdoch and Elmer Kolbe. I just couldn't bring myself to believe that Elmer would want me out of town. Of course, the mayor could have gotten to him.

In my mind, the two people who wanted me out of town the most were the mayor and Eleanore. "I'll be back," I said suddenly.

"Where are you going?" Rudy asked.

"I'm going to visit Elmer."

Twenty-Eight

Elmer was at the firehouse, the very place I knew he would be, since he was the fire chief, after all. The firehouse was an old building, and an early-twentieth-century fire truck sat on the front lawn. The antique fire engine had actually been used here in this town, and Elmer had had the presence of mind to keep it and restore it. I went in, passed the front desk, and went down the hall to his office.

"Torie," he said. "Come in."

He didn't seem to be hiding any nefarious doings with that bright smile. It was the same smile I'd seen on his face my whole life. To believe he was faking it meant he'd been faking it all that time, and that was far too disturbing for me to think about.

"I've got a question for you, Elmer," I said. I took the seat across from his desk.

"What is it?"

"Did you attend the box social at the Methodist church?"

"Which one?"

"The last one."

"Yes," he said. "I was there."

"Was there anybody there who was not a member of your church?"

"Sure," he said and shrugged. "Lots."

I wasn't sure what to ask next, and it turned out I needn't have worried about it, because he posed the next question. "Why? You seem agitated."

"Have you seen the papers today?"

Rubbing his forehead, he sat back and exhaled for what seemed like a full minute. "Yes," he said.

"Do you believe the story?" I asked.

He said nothing.

"Do you believe I said those things?"

"No, Torie. Even if you meant those things it would be political suicide to actually have said them. I would believe Eleanore capable of shooting herself in the foot, but not you."

"Oh, I've shot my own foot before," I said.

"Yes, but Torie, this would be like blowing your damn foot right off your leg. You wouldn't be that stupid," he said.

"Then you know what I'm getting at here," I said. "Elmer, somebody is trying to make life so difficult for me that I'll leave town, or at the very least disappear from the public scene."

"I know."

"They tried beating me up," I said, "but that didn't work. They went after my family—whether or not they would have actually hurt my kids, I don't know—and now defamation of character. What is going on?"

"I wish I knew," he said. His small eyes narrowed. He played steeple with his fingers and then leaned forward. "Why did you ask about the box social?"

"Because Eleanore said that was where the anti-Torie campaign began. I've looked at the list of church members. Aside from Eleanore, I can find no outright enemies of mine on that list."

"I'm on that list," he said.

"Yes, you are."

"You suspect me?"

"No," I said. "Can you remember anything unusual about that box social?"

"Not really," he said. "Eleanore was there—she hung with a pretty snotty group that day. I can't really remember anything sticking out in my mind. Just that there was an air of . . . discontent."

"Great," I said. I squeezed my eyes and tried to make my headache go away.

"What is it?" he asked. "There's something you're not saying."

"The mayor—" I began.

"He goes to the Catholic church, I think. And no, he wasn't there."

"No, I mean . . . He hasn't said anything to you about me, has he?"

"He's always talking about you," he said.

"Oh, that's comforting," I said. "I meant in an official capacity."

"You mean, has he bribed me to slander you? You know, threatened to pull some strings so that I'd lose my job if I didn't cooperate? That sort of thing?"

"That's not how I mean it to sound," I said.

He stared at me long and hard. I wilted beneath the intensity. He was my elder. The man was in his seventies. He refused to retire, even when everybody told him he should. I felt like I was being scolded by my grandfather and he hadn't even spoken a single word. "He did, actually," Elmer said, "but I told him to jump in the river. It's only a few hundred yards from his house. It should be easy enough for him to find."

My mouth went dry at his announcement. "Oh, my God," I said.

"Torie, this was a very long time ago. Two or three years ago. Long before all of this stuff came up with Sylvia," he said.

"So he could have been waiting to play his hand," I said. The hysteria rose in my voice like mercury in a thermometer.

"Nobody knew you were going to inherit everything," Elmer said.

"No, but still, maybe that was just icing on the cake. Maybe he was going to make this move regardless, and Sylvia dying just made it easier for him," I said.

"Torie," Elmer said, "talk to your stepdad first. Don't go off half cocked and accuse Bill of anything."

"I won't," I said. I stood then, not sure how to end this conversation. "I . . . thanks, Elmer."

"No problem," he said. "Let me know when you need me to come back for the tours."

I smiled, knowing that Elmer understood. "I will."

•

On the way back to the Gaheimer House, I unexpectedly ran into Eleanore Murdoch. I tried to pretend I didn't see her. In fact, I ducked behind a small fig tree and went about picking some imaginary gum off my shoe. But you know, nothing gets past Eleanore. Not a damn thing.

"Oh, Torie," she said. "I thought that was you."

"Eleanore," I said. I took a deep breath. Surprisingly, she was dressed down today. She wore black leotard pants with a purple sweater that came down to her knees, which only accentuated the fact that the woman's shoulders are three times wider than her hips. It wasn't her appearance that bothered me so much as her attitude. It was as if nothing had transpired at the meeting at all. She thought she was going to schmooze me and I'd forget all about how she darn near incited a riot in my name this week. "Is there something you wanted?"

A dead person could not possibly have mistaken my greeting for anything other than the cold shoulder, but Eleanore—as I have spent a lifetime discovering—is as dense as the fog on Venus. "What band do you have lined up for tomorrow?"

"It's none of your business," I said and proceeded to walk past her.

"Wait just a minute," she said. "Who do you think you're talking to?"

"Well, you look like the two-faced, bigmouthed idiot who was at the historical society meeting the other night. You know, the woman who kept referring to me as *that* woman," I said. "Really, Eleanore. If you're going to plant the seeds of hatred, you have to be prepared to reap whatever ugly plant you sow."

"Well, I never," she said.

"Neither have I." I turned to leave, and then I happened to think of the words Father Bingham had said to me about how I should forgive and love those who don't necessarily have my well-being in mind—and for once, I really looked at Eleanore with the blinders off. Freeing myself of all the pettiness made me see her for what she really was: a pathetic woman who was so unhappy with herself that she had to spend her life pretending she had a life. Or that she had somebody else's life.

I don't know. Maybe it's because *How the Grinch Stole Christmas* is my favorite Dr. Seuss book and my favorite Christmas story, but somehow it seemed as if my heart grew three sizes bigger standing on the street staring up at this giant woman with a beehive hairdo and Oreo cookie earrings. I couldn't stand it one more minute. I lunged at her and gave her the biggest hug I could muster.

"I forgive you, Eleanore. I don't care how petty you get, how mean you get, or how jealous of me you get, I'm not going to care anymore."

"What?" she said.

Ahh, if only I'd had a camera to register the look on her face.

"You need to let all that go. Look deep inside you, Eleanore. I'm sure there's a beautiful person somewhere in there, just waiting to be released. You know, like a butterfly from its cocoon."

"Have you lost your mind?"

"No, I haven't. I'll tell you what, Eleanore. You throw whatever you want at me. You go right on ahead, because deep down inside, I know that you're just doing it because you feel wholly inadequate. So if you want to remove me from power, go ahead. Try. But remember, I'll always be here for you."

With that, I smiled and left a completely and totally—for the

first time ever—speechless Eleanore Murdoch standing on the sidewalk.

Life seemed suddenly good.

Well, except that there was still somebody out there trying to
get rid of me. And my chickens could be in serious danger by
nightfall.

Twenty-Nine

I went back to the Gaheimer House to find that Rudy had eaten two of the three sandwiches. Helen had gone home. Deputy Miller was in the kitchen, watching the news on Sylvia's old black-and-white television.

"I can't believe you ate two sandwiches," I said.

"I saved you one."

"Yes, but—" I sighed. Like it mattered. "Why don't you go on back to my mother's? I'm sure she's got something wonderful cooked."

"Why? What are you going to do?"

"I've got some digging to do," I said. "I have to find a connection between Sylvia and an unhappy resident of New Kassel."

"Just walk down the street," he said. "Any street."

"No, there's something I'm missing."

"Torie," Rudy said, "you could spend every night for the next two years digging through the papers in this house and still not find what you're looking for. More than likely it'll be an accidental thing."

"I know, but I have to try."

He rolled his eyes and sighed with exasperation. Yes, I know, being married to me is a trial. He leaned in and kissed me. "My mother will be back tomorrow."

"Is she going to stay with us at my mother's?"

"Maybe."

"Oh," I said. See how good I was being? I could have said something really nasty, but I refrained.

"You haven't gone back on your whole 'I was a jerk' thing, have you?"

"No, no," I said. "I was a jerk. I intend to apologize."

"Okay, call me when you're finished here and I'll come get you."

"Well, I might just stay until Miller goes home. I'll ride into Wisteria with him."

"All right. See you then."

"Oh, but go by and check on the chickens. I've got horrible visions of *Chicken Run* flashing through my head."

He kissed me through laughter and then left for my mother's house in Wisteria. I fetched myself a Dr Pepper and sat down at my desk. The first thing I was going to do was check every reference I had for Mayor Castlereagh and his family. I hauled out all the family history charts and files that Sylvia had spent a lifetime collecting on the residents of this town. I had compiled a great deal of data in the computer, but not all of it, so I grabbed the paper files. I'd have to do this the old-fashioned way.

The mayor had been born one William Jarvis Castlereagh in July 1949. Bill was the middle child of three boys. His father and grandfather were born here. His mother was from Kansas. He was the father of four children. One of them arrived seven months after the date of his wedding, but Karri was born premature, not conceived prematurely. At least that is the story Mrs. Castlereagh tells everybody within ten minutes of meeting them. Okay, so they didn't wait until their honeymoon. That was hardly a crime and definitely had nothing to do with me.

Yada, yada, yada. Nothing. The only things I could find that were the least bit out of the ordinary were some probate records, and the only reason they were out of the ordinary was that I hadn't known about them.

He and his wife had already bought and paid for their cemetery plots in the Santa Lucia Cemetery. Two rows over from Sylvia. I suppose it wasn't all that odd for somebody fairly young to have already purchased a burial plot, but it weirded me out. I personally wouldn't want to make that kind of decision early on. What if I changed my mind? What if that nice peaceful cemetery became surrounded by factories and such thirty years from now? I might not want to spend eternity next to a smokestack. Not that it matters. I worry about the stupidest things.

Well, that was all I could find in our genealogical files. That didn't mean there wasn't anything to be found among Sylvia's personal papers. I flipped through some of the records and found Eleanore's family charts. I always forgot that she and Chuck Velasco were second cousins. Something I'm sure Chuck would love to forget as well.

The phone rang, and I answered it. It was Colin. "Hey, I talked with Danny Eisenbach. It appears as though he told at least four people about Mike Walker."

"Great."

"Within an hour, half the town could have known about your private investigator."

"Who did he tell?"

"He told Virgie Burgermeister, for one. The mayor, for another."

"Oh, this just gets better and better."

"Claims he even told Duran."

"Great."

"I also talked to Virgie and Harold about the restraining order."

"And?"

"It seems as though Harold did lunge at Sylvia and try to punch her. She insulted his mother. He flat-out said, let me quote here, 'Ain't nobody insults my mama.' So there you have it."

"Dead end."

"Not necessarily," he said, "but nothing that I can arrest anybody for."

Somehow none of this made me feel any better. I banged my head on my desk and then took a drink of my soda.

Colin said, "However, we did get a good footprint from under the tree in your front yard."

"Of?"

"I think it's our perp."

"Cool."

"Yeah, now we just have to compare it to, oh, a thousand or so feet."

"Well, you'll have plenty to keep you busy."

"Right," he said. "What's going on with you?"

"Oh, nothing," I said.

"I'll check in later. Call me if you find anything."

"I will."

He hung up, and I went back to searching through the pile on my desk. Bill was also remotely related to Eleanore. Actually, it was through Eleanore's husband, Oscar. Oscar Murdoch, according to his charts—and I knew it was true—was related to Helen Wickland's mother, Constance Trotter. I glanced at Helen's five-generation chart. Helen was born in 1957 as Helen Renee Trotter. Her mother had been only fifteen years old and unmarried. Helen had mentioned this to me before in passing, and I never felt comfortable inquiring further since she had not volunteered any more about it. Not that a person's reluctance to talk ever stopped me from enquiring before, but Helen was a friend and it seemed to make her uncomfortable, so I didn't push it. Constance Trotter was the daughter of William Trotter and . . .

I nearly knocked over my soda can.

William Trotter had been married to one Mildred Blaine O'Shaughnessy.

I'll be a son-of-a-gun. Mildred O'Shaughnessy was born in New York City in 1924. Married William Trotter in 1940 in Cedar Rapids, Iowa. According to Helen's charts, William died in 1943, one year after Constance was born. So a young and widowed Millie O'Shaughnessy Trotter moved to New Kassel, Missouri, where Sylvia just happened to live.

I searched the file cabinet of my mind, trying to remember if Sylvia or Wilma or anybody had ever mentioned a connection to Helen's family. I came up blank. Helen had had the same relationship with Sylvia that half the town had—cordial and superficial.

Could it be that Sylvia just happened to have some of the Trotter family things to put in a collection? A lot of people donated one-of-a-kind heirloom letters and diaries to the historical society because they didn't necessarily want the items but knew they were of historical importance. Could that be how Sylvia got the postcard? But that wouldn't explain the letter written to Sylvia by Father Kincaid. He had been speaking of Mrs. O'Shaughnessy, who must have been Mildred's mother. So no, these were Sylvia's letters, not a donation. But I still didn't understand.

And what did any of it have to do with me?

I suppose everything didn't have to be about me.

I scanned the chart. Mildred's parents were down as Theodora Wentz of Albany, New York, who died in New York City in 1927, and Robert O'Shaughnessy from County Kerry in Ireland, who died in 1926. Millie had indeed been an orphan.

I walked down to Sylvia's old office and pulled a few books off the shelf. Old yearbooks. As far as I knew, Sylvia had lived her entire life right here in this little corner of eastern Missouri. Most of her professional life had been here, too. The only place she could have become acquainted with somebody who lived and died in New York would have been in school—if not in college, then in high school or grade school, although that was less likely.

I thumbed through Sylvia's college books and found what I was looking for. Theodora Wentz had attended college with Sylvia Pershing.

"Hey, Miller!"

"Yeah?" he called from the kitchen.

"I'm going over to Helen's house," I said. "I'll be right back."

"Sure thing," he said.

I walked across the street and down a block or so until I came to Helen's house. I knocked on the door, and she answered within a few seconds, holding a pot holder and a very large burnt duck on a fork. "Want some dinner?" she asked.

"No, thank you," I said. "I was wondering if I could speak with you?"

"Certainly," she said. "Come on in. Let me just get rid of this dead bird."

I stepped inside Helen's living room and had to laugh as I saw the black smoke pouring from the kitchen. The fire alarm blared from somewhere down the hall, and her husband was running around fanning the ceiling with a towel. "She insists on these exotic dishes," he said.

I laughed, and she returned from the kitchen, drying her hands on a towel. "What can I do for you?"

I pulled the postcard out and handed it to her.

"Oh, my God," she said. "That's my grandmother. Where did you get this?"

"Turn it over," I said.

She turned it over and read the single line: *I think you have forgotten your promise.* Her eyebrows knit together in confusion. "I don't understand."

"It's addressed to Sylvia."

The color drained from her face then, as she slowly handed the card back to me.

"Look, Helen," I said. "I have never pushed you about . . . your mother or any of the rest of your family history."

"My mother was fifteen when she had me. She didn't happen to get a good look at my father. It was kind of dark," she said.

"I'm so sorry," I said.

She crossed her arms. "What is it you want?"

"What was the promise, Helen?"

She shrugged.

"Surely you've heard stories. You've asked questions."

"Believe it or not, Torie, not everybody talks about their past. Not everybody is descended from Charlemagne and is a Daughter of the American Revolution."

"Look, I've got my share of horse thieves and murderers," I said. "Don't get defensive."

"Yes, but your parents are perfect," she said.

"Oh, right. Have I introduced you to my sister? My half sister who was born while my parents were still married?"

She rolled her eyes.

"Don't give me that crap, Helen. What was the promise?"

"Why do you care?"

"Because . . . because I just do. I care. I can't help it. Just when I think I have Sylvia figured out, she morphs on me. She's like that Odo guy on *Deep Space Nine*."

"So this is to make you feel better?" she asked. I was a bit taken aback by the venom. Helen and I had been friends for years. Of course, her reluctance to stick up for me at the historical society meeting had floored me, too.

"Are you . . . Helen, are you upset that Sylvia left me everything?" The bottom fell out of my stomach as I suddenly realized that Helen had been acting strange lately.

A tear ran down her cheek.

Oh, dear Lord! Was it Helen who had beaten me with a baseball bat during the Strawberry Festival? Could she have thrown the rocks at my house? But why?

"Helen, we've been friends a long time," I said. "Please, tell me what the promise was."

"My great-grandmother found out in the spring of 1926 that she had consumption. Her husband had recently died, but I'm not sure from what," Helen said. "She wrote to Sylvia—I'm still not real clear how they knew each other—but she wrote to Sylvia and asked if she would take care of her daughter if she died. Her daughter, Millie, was my grandmother."

I closed my eyes as the tears came to the edge.

"According to my mother, Sylvia had agreed, but then a family in Philadelphia said they would take her. Sylvia thought that would be better, since she wasn't married. She thought my grandmother would be better off with a mother and a father, instead of just her."

"Can you blame her for that?" I asked.

"No," she said.

"So how did your grandma end up here?"

"The couple that took her in Philadelphia died in a fire, just six months later. The nuns at the orphanage contacted Sylvia. This time, she was more reluctant," Helen said and swiped at a tear. "I don't know if she suddenly realized that she'd make a shitty parent or if she just didn't want to be bothered."

"But how did Millie end up in Iowa?" I asked.

Helen looked taken aback at first. Then she smiled. "You really are good at your job."

"I can fill in the where and the when. It's the why that gives me the most trouble. Unless somebody from the past decides to speak," I said.

"One of the priests found her a home in Iowa, and according to my grandmother he came with her to Iowa on the train. But when they got there, the family had recently given birth to twins. They decided they couldn't afford another mouth," Helen said, "so my grandmother was stuck."

Thus the last-ditch effort to contact Sylvia. "I think you have forgotten your promise," I whispered. The tears spilled down my face. How could she have done this? How could Sylvia have turned this child out into the cold?

"I don't know exactly what happened, but my grandmother ran away. Somewhere in the next several years she met my grandfather and they got married. But bad luck seemed to follow Millie: He died a few years later, just after my mother was born. By that point, she was pregnant again. Millie was desperate to take care of her children, so she came to New Kassel," Helen said. "I don't know if she thought Sylvia would welcome her and take her in or what."

"So what happened?"

"As far as I know, Sylvia never acknowledged who she was. I'm not even sure if my grandmother told her who she was. She was Mildred Trotter then, not Millie O'Shaughnessy."

"Oh, my God," I said.

"Sylvia did give her a job, though," Helen said. "My grandmother became Sylvia's laundress."

I cupped my mouth with my hand as more tears spilled over. "Ms. Trotter. Of course, I remember her."

"But I suppose the trend was set for my family by that point."

"Oh, Helen," I said.

"Save your tears, Torie," she said. "I'm long over it."

"But the Gaheimer House . . . the money. It should all be yours," I said.

"I suppose, technically, if Sylvia had raised my grandmother. Yes, it would be mine and my brother's. But she didn't raise her. And she gave her nothing."

My knees were actually weak from Helen's words. My chest burned from trying not to cry. I don't know why I tried so hard; the tears were still streaming down my face no matter what I did.

"I hate to be the one to shatter your illusion of the great Sylvia," Helen said. "But you asked."

"Thank you. I . . . I have to go," I said. "I'll talk to you later, Helen."

I all but ran from her house, wiping at tears and gasping for air. I fumbled in my pocket and pulled out my cell phone. I dialed Colin's number in the dark—thank God for speed dial—and waited for him to answer. "Colin, it's me, Torie."

"What's the matter?" he asked.

I sobbed and wiped my face. "I . . . I think it might be Helen," I said. "I think she might be the one who's been trying to . . . hurt me."

"Torie, are you all right?" he asked.

"I'm fine," I said. Okay, my heart was broken and I would never be the same again, but I wasn't bleeding to death. "Look, I just came from her house. It's a long story. But maybe you could get some fibers from her. Check her shoes. She's got a reason, Colin. She has a damn good reason for wanting revenge."

"I'll get right on it," he said. "Do you need me to come get you?"

"No," I said. I hung up the phone and fumbled my way to the Gaheimer House. "Miller?" I said as I entered the house.

Surprisingly, he wasn't there. I found a note on the table saying he had to go because of an accident on 55. I set the alarm, shut the door, and sat down on the step and cried some more. I wondered if the world would ever be right again. I could understand Sylvia not wanting to take in a child, especially if she thought she would not be a good parent. But to promise somebody she'd take care of her child and then renege? I couldn't make it right in my mind. No matter how I looked at it, I could not forgive Sylvia for this.

Then it started to rain.

A car pulled up in front of the house, and Duran opened the door. "My God, Torie. What's the matter? Are you all right?"

"Wh-what are you doing here?"

"I was just coming from Chuck's. Leigh felt like pizza. I couldn't say no to her," he said.

"Oh, that's nice."

"Are you okay? Why are you crying?"

"I just . . . Can you take me home?"

"Of course," he said. He came over to the porch and gave me his hand to take, which I gladly did. I walked toward his car in a complete daze.

He opened the door. I got in, wiped my face on my sleeve, and vowed never to cry another tear over Sylvia Pershing as long as I lived.

Thirty

So why are you so upset?" Duran asked.

"Long story," I said. I glanced into the backseat at the pizza from Chuck's and my stomach rumbled. Even if I'm not hungry, pizza from Velasco's will make my mouth water and my stomach rumble.

"Am I taking you to Wisteria?"

"Yeah, my mom's house. Or, well, Colin's house. However you look at it," I said.

"Is it weird having him for a stepfather?"

"Unfair is more like it. Not weird."

He laughed. My nose continued to run. "Hey, have you got a tissue?"

"In the glove box."

I opened the glove box and found a tiny package of tissues. I hated to use them, since there were so few left, but I'd already wiped tears all over my sleeves; I wasn't about to wipe snot, too. My fingers fumbled and I dropped the Kleenex on the floor. I reached down to pick it up.

In the dark I felt around. My hand brushed something round and hard.

A baseball bat.

I had not been able to find Sylvia's bat since the day I was attacked.

Calm down. Think. Duran was a jock. He probably played softball in a league or something. For God's sake, this was Deputy Duran we were talking about.

"Hey, can you turn on the light?" I said. "I dropped the Kleenex and can't find it."

He flipped on the overhead light, filling the car with that odd yellowish glow, and I leaned my head between my knees and looked at the end of the bat poking out from under the seat. Scribbled in marker was the year 1985.

This was Sylvia's baseball bat.

Suddenly my mind started replaying the events of the past week. Things began crowding into my head.

"Did you find them?" he asked.

"Yeah," I said and grabbed the tissues.

He flipped off the light. "So why are you so upset?"

"Oh, it's just difficult when you find out that the people you love aren't who they claim to be."

He made a clicking sound with his teeth. "Don't I know it."

A box social where there was a consensus that you should be removed from power. Edwin and Leigh Duran attended the Methodist church. What were the odds they attended the box social?

"So, you and Leigh do much with your church?" Only after I said it did I think that it might have sounded like it came out of left field. Maybe he wouldn't notice.

"Yeah, every now and then."

"Where do you go?"

"The Methodist church."

"Oh, I heard they had a box social not too long ago."

"Yeah," he said. "We went to that. It was nice."

He's been short on cash. Colin's words echoed hollowly in my head, as if the world had no bass, only treble. Duran needed money. I now had money. Lots of money.

Who was sitting right next to Eleanore Murdoch during the historical society meeting that turned into a witch hunt? Leigh Duran. Sitting there telling Eleanore what to say, whom to elect. What's more, who had been nominated for president and didn't win? Leigh Duran.

Hell, he even told Duran. Danny Eisenbach had told Duran that I had hired a private investigator.

It made my head hurt to think about it. Who had access? Who was so careful not to leave any fingerprints or footprints in the secret stairway? Somebody who would have thought of it. Quite a few people might think not to leave fingerprints, but almost nobody would think about footprints! Unless it was somebody who was trained to think about it.

I used to do favors for her all the time.

Somebody who thought Sylvia owed him. For whatever reason his twisted little mind had come up with, Duran thought he was owed something by Sylvia. But I could not figure out how he thought he would actually get it, even if I were out of the picture.

I tried to keep my breathing regular as I sat in the seat next to him. All I had to do was get to my mother's house and I could call Colin, and everything would be fine. Duran had no reason whatsoever to think that I suspected him of anything.

Wait, stop. What was I thinking? Was I really so paranoid that now I thought anybody and everybody was out to get me? Was Duran really capable of this?

He did have the baseball bat in his car.

True, but maybe he wanted a souvenir of Sylvia and didn't have the nerve to come right out and ask for one. So he took it. He took it; that didn't mean that he used it.

And I had to remind myself that he could have killed me. He could have killed Mike Walker. But he didn't. What was it Colin had said? Mike had been attacked by somebody who couldn't quite follow through with murder.

"You're awfully quiet," Duran said.

"I'm really exhausted. And I'm really upset," I said. "Don't take it personally."

"My wife gets real quiet when she's upset," he said. "I think it sort of runs in her family."

"What is Leigh's maiden name?" I asked. The very first question every respectable genealogist would ask somebody. The maiden name—the surname—told you a lot about a person. It told you ethnicity. Sometimes you could figure out what region a woman came from just by her maiden name. Sometimes you could even get an idea of religion. Like O'Shea, for example. It said that Rudy was Irish, and either Catholic or Protestant. I would automatically know to scratch Muslim off the list with a name like that.

"Franklin," he said. "And as far as I know, she's not related to old Ben." He laughed at his own joke.

Franklin. Franklin. I ran the name through my mental file. Was there anybody I knew named Franklin? Did it matter? Not really. I was simply trying to keep him talking long enough to get me home without him realizing I had discovered the bat.

Just then my phone rang. I nearly screamed and jumped off of the seat as I scrambled in my pocket for it. "Hello?"

"Torie, it's Colin."

"Hi, Colin," I said. I smiled and made sure I said it loud enough that Deputy Duran could hear it. In a flash, I had figured it out. One of Sylvia's nieces had married a Franklin. Julie. Julie Pershing had married Steve Franklin! Could it be that Leigh Franklin Duran was Sylvia's great-great-niece? Had it even occurred to Colin to check out Sylvia's great-great-nieces and -nephews—the third generation—or had he only checked attitudes and alibis for the second? I wasn't so sure I would have thought of it.

And Leigh Duran had just attempted suicide. What if this had nothing to do with the money and had everything to do with revenge?

"I've got a team that's going to collect fibers and stuff from Helen in just a few minutes."

"All right," I said.

"But I need to ask you something."

"What?"

"The night after the historical society meeting . . ."

"Yeah?" I said. The palms of my hands were sweating so badly that I nearly dropped the phone. I swallowed hard.

"Did you ask Duran to come by and check out the house?"

"Mmmm, I don't think so. Not the night after. Why?"

"Well, Mike Walker came to," he said. "I had checked Mr. Walker's logs before but didn't think much of it, but when I questioned him over the phone, he said that the only person who went in or out of the Gaheimer House during nonbusiness hours was Duran. So I was wondering if maybe you'd asked him to do some moonlighting that I didn't know about."

"No," I said. "I could ask him, though."

Dead silence on the line.

"Are you with Duran?" he asked.

"Yes, he's driving me home."

Come on, Colin, quit being such a twit.

"Is everything all right?" he asked.

"Nope."

"Torie, are you in danger?"

"Not yet, you moron."

Duran turned and laughed at me. He probably was wishing that he could call his boss a moron and get by with it. I laughed right along with him and pretended everything was just fine.

"You've found something that already brought you to this con-clusion," he said.

"Give the man a prize."

"All right, ask Duran what he did with the files on the Jenkins case."

"Huh?"

"You said you could ask him. He's going to want to know what I want you to ask him. So ask him about the Jenkins file so he doesn't get suspicious."

I relayed the message.

"On my desk," Duran answered.

"On his desk," I said.

"I'm just going to stay on the phone with you until he pulls into my driveway and you're safe and sound," he said.

Oh, wonderful. What if Bat Boy decided to pull over and kill me? What was I supposed to do, cell phone him to death? "All right," I said. "Boy, it's dark on the Outer Road."

"Outer Road. Got it. I'll have Miller find you guys and tail you," Colin said.

"Sure, whatever." I could hear Colin speaking into his radio, giving orders to find and follow a blue Buick Century headed west on the Outer Road.

Just then a cat ran out into the middle of the road and Duran slammed on his brakes. When he did, the baseball bat shot forward and in between my feet. He flipped the overhead light on, I'm assuming to see if everything was all right. I watched in slow motion as his gaze fell between my feet and landed on the baseball bat. I looked down and then up to meet his eyes, and he knew that I knew.

"Shit," I said.

"Torie? Are you compromised?" Colin's voice came across that thin lifeline that was my cell phone.

"And how," I said into the phone.

"It's not what you think," Duran said. "I . . . I found it and I didn't think it would hurt, you know, to take it out of the house."

"Oh, shit," Colin said as he heard what Duran was saying. "Torie, you need to get out of that car."

At that moment Duran must have realized that I suspected him of a whole lot more than just swiping a bat from Sylvia's house. He opened his door, grabbed my phone, and threw it out into the night. I reached for my seat belt, but he grabbed my hair in his fist. His wristwatch snagged my hair and I cried out, but I managed to unlock the seat belt. I didn't think he would have heard it click, since I had been screaming at that moment. "Think, Edwin. Colin knows I'm with you! Think about what you're doing!"

"Shit!" he yelled. "It wasn't suppposed to happen like this. You just couldn't give up and leave town, could you?"

"Edwin, calm down," I said. My hands were up in the air. See? Total surrender. No threat whatsoever. If only I could make him believe that. If he thought for one minute I was any kind of threat, there was no telling what he would do. He was a desperate man. He was caught and he knew it. Now he had to make a choice. He either had to leave it be and let me out of the car—and face some jail time, not to mention losing his job—or he had to take it to the next level. By the look on his face, he was contemplating his fate.

"If you kill me, you have to run. If you run, you lose everything anyway. You may as well let me go and face the music," I said. He yanked my hair a little harder, and I bent my body with him to try to lessen the resistance on my scalp.

"I can't go to jail."

"Edwin, think about this!"

"A cop in jail? I am thinking about it!"

"Come on, Edwin," I said. An unexpected sob escaped from my throat. My stomach burned with fear. Even my toes were numb. "I've got three kids to raise."

It's funny how even at that moment all I could think of was my kids.

"Get out of the car," he said and let go of my hair. He reached down and pulled the bat out from under the seat.

I nearly vomited right then and there. I squeezed my eyes shut. *There's no place like home. There's no place like home.* This could not be happening. I thought briefly about begging, literally getting down on my hands and knees and begging him to let me go. Then I got angry instead. Who did this twerp think he was?

"Fine," I said. I shoved the car door open and got out. I could hear the creek across the road. The creek that meandered through the woods and ran right by the fishing shack. By the entrance to the tunnel. "Come on, you sack of shit. Let's get this over with."

Duran came around the front of the car. "What did you just say?"

"I can't stand people like you. Think you're entitled to the whole damn world! When something doesn't go your way, you run to your mama and cry, and then you take what isn't yours."

"Sylvia should have left me something!"

"Well, no, actually, last time I checked, your wife is the one who's related to Sylvia. Not you."

He clenched his teeth and gripped the handle of the bat like I'd seen Mark McGwire do a hundred times. "I've paid enough rent on that house, it should be mine by now! But no, Sylvia just kept holding on to it. I did favors for her any time she asked. Anytime she heard a noise, I'd stop by. 'Is there anything else I can do for you, Sylvia? Can I get you anything, Sylvia?' And still she took that damn rent check from me every month, all the while knowing I'd already paid for the house!" He slammed the bat into the headlight of his car. "I put up with that bitchy old woman, thinking she'd finally give me my house. And she never did."

"This is about a house, Duran? Jesus." I felt his car with my hands as I backed up a few steps.

"No, it's not about the house. It's about you. You getting everything my wife should have had. You strut around this town like an undeclared queen, you take and take from people, and then who gets the dough when the old lady kicks the bucket? Her living relatives? Not hardly," he said and smashed his window. "Who is Sylvia's confidant? My wife? No. Who gets the job in the pretty dresses? Is it Leigh? No. Who is the chairperson of the events committee? Who is president of the historical society? Who has three perfectly healthy children? You, you, you!" The baseball bat whizzed through the air as he smashed it into the hood of his car.

"Edwin . . . it's not like that."

"'Oh, I just haven't gotten used to the fact that I'm a landlady.'" He mimicked the words I had spoken to him in the Gaheimer House that day. "Like you weren't planning to be queen of New Kassel from the very beginning. All the while, Leigh just kept waiting for her chance. Her chance at your scraps!"

"God, Edwin, I didn't know."

"Would it have mattered?"

He took another step and I backed up three. When I reached the back of his car I turned and took off running across the road and into the woods. It was so dark I could barely see my hand in front of my face, but as long as I kept the creek to my right, I would get where I wanted to go. I didn't look back. I assumed Duran was following me, but I wasn't about to give up the millisecond it would take to look back over my shoulder and find out.

A tree branch smacked me in the face and I veered off course, twisting my ankle in a rabbit hole. Within a few minutes I had come to the fishing shack and my own rabbit hole. *Go on, Alice, Go down the hole.*

I pulled open the doors on the tunnel and ran down the stairs. My shoes were slick from running through the woods, and I slid down the stairs as if I were on a surfboard as I heard the doors bang shut behind me. I ended up on the floor, in utter and complete darkness.

Don't panic. I was trying to remain calm, but no matter what I said to myself, my breathing came in huge ragged gasps. I felt along the side for the wall of the tunnel. I found it and managed to stand. Okay, I was touching the wall. So I was standing. I knew up from down now. But I still couldn't control my breathing. If I didn't see light soon, I would burst.

I ran along the tunnel, never letting my hand leave the wall. If I lost the wall, I would lose myself.

Then I heard the bang of the doors above me.

Duran had anticipated my destination. Well, at least I didn't have to wonder if he was following me or not. The good news was that he seemed to be fumbling in the dark as much as I was. He had no flashlight. He probably had one in the car, but he hadn't taken the time to get it before taking off after me. So he was as blind as I was. On the other hand, he knew the tunnel better than I did.

There was only one thing I could think of to do. If he was using the walls to guide himself like I was, then I just had to figure out which side of the wall he would use. I was right handed, and yet I had used my left hand to feel my way through, I suppose so my right hand could be free. But how could I know Duran would do the same thing? How could I even know if he'd use the wall to guide him at all? I had to assume he would. It was pitch dark. There was no way anybody could make it through this tunnel without following the wall.

I reached my right hand out and crossed over to the other side. Then I lay down on the floor of the tunnel, trying very hard not to think of the multilegged things that lived in here. *Just please, God, no spiders!* I could handle anything but spiders. I lay down, horizontal, as close to the wall as I could get, and hoped that when Duran went by he would miss me.

I got lucky. He, too, was using the left side of the tunnel. I could hear him as he went by me, his feet scuffing along, his breathing uneven. Then I heard a *swoosh* sound as the bat came darting through the air. He must have been swinging the bat randomly, thinking that I might be standing next to him. He never thought that I'd be on the ground.

When he was past me, I stood up slowly and headed back toward the entrance of the tunnel, back toward the fishing shack, feeling my way along the wall as I went. I reached the steps sooner than I thought I would and tripped up them. I hit my chin on a step as I landed, and stars burst into view.

Well, I said I wanted light. I had light.

I lay there on the steps a few seconds, simply because I could not move. The combination of the hit to my chin and the fact that I couldn't tell up from down finally took its toll. I vomited all over the stairs and myself. Somewhere in the back of my mind I knew that Duran was going to hear all the noise I was making and turn around and come back for me.

The next thing I knew, the door to the tunnel opened, a light whipped by my eyes, and what seemed like a giant hand reached in and pulled me out. "Torie?"

It was Rudy.

Rudy?

"What are you doing here?" I said. I climbed up the stairs with his help and collapsed onto him. Fear engulfed me. If Duran came back, he'd kill us both. Then my children wouldn't have any parents. I immediately began crying, sobs ripping from me as I clung to his shirt. I could barely stand up. My paralysis was due more to fear than anything else.

Rudy flashed the light at the forest floor, and two very large feet came into view. I followed them to find my stepfather standing there looking pissed off and menacing beyond belief. "Where is the son-of-a-bitch?"

"He went down . . . the . . . tunnel," I managed. "He's headed for the house."

Colin spoke into his radio. "Newsome. He's headed your way."

Thirty-One

Saturday. The Strawberry Festival. The band played onstage. Tobias Thorley stood on the corner in his knickers that were too big for his little wiry body, playing his accordion and smiling his big toothy grin. The smell of Kettle Korn wafted through the air, mixing with the aromas of funnel cakes and cotton candy. Laughter. Cheering. Cash registers ringing.

I stood on the steps of the Gaheimer House, unable to move.

"Torie?" Colin said. My mother was with him, looking peaceful and radiant in her new red blouse, smiling up from her position in the wheelchair. It was a hopeful smile. Hopeful of what, I wasn't sure.

My sister stepped out of the building and stood next to me.

"What?" I said to Colin.

"Have you heard anything I said?" he said.

"Yes."

"They found that sapphire ring you were asking about, along with some antiques and a few other items, at Duran's house," he said. He handed the ring to me. "Will you be okay?"

After placing the ring on my finger, I hugged myself close. I wasn't sure I would ever be okay. "How did Duran know about the tunnel?" I asked.

"Helen told him."

My eyes cut around and met his for the first time in our conversation. "Helen knew about the tunnel?"

"Her grandmother found it when she worked for Sylvia. Evidently, she told Helen about it, and Helen passed that knowledge on to a few people in a drinking game once. It was when she was very young."

I shrugged. I couldn't believe I had never heard about the tunnel.

"They, of course, didn't know why the tunnel had been built. You figured that part out."

"Why didn't Helen ever ask me about it?"

"I guess she would have had to divulge a lot more to you if she had told you about the tunnel."

"So has Duran admitted to killing Sylvia?"

"Torie, Sylvia died in her sleep. Duran said he never hurt her. He only tried to scare her a few times. A power thing. He got off on making the all-powerful Sylvia Pershing scared. He says he didn't kill her," he said.

"And you believe him?" I asked.

"The only way I can tell for certain is to exhume the body. Do you want to do that?"

"No," I said. "I guess not."

"She was old. She died. And apparently the assault that she endured back in the seventies was totally unrelated to this. Sylvia had enemies."

And how.

Would I end up like that? Hated by everybody?

I looked down at the ground. "Mom?"

"Yeah?" There I went, doing what Mary did to me all the time. I couldn't speak to her without saying, "Mom?" first.

"The other day, when we were at Pierre's, you gave me the funniest look when Sally Huber came up to the table. Why?"

Mom looked away and then back at me. "How long have you known Sally Huber?"

"Forever. We used to play in the sandbox together. I was with her when they found her dog dead by the river. We sat at the same table at prom. Why?"

Mom smiled at me. Not a condescending smile, but not a happy smile, either. "Then why did you sit up straight, wipe your mouth, and act so professional when she came over to the table?"

"I . . . I didn't realize I did."

"Yes, you did. It's because you own her house now. You're her landlady. You expected her to treat you differently, so you treated her differently right off the bat. You didn't give her a chance. You intimidated her," she said. "I just thought it was funny. You know, Sylvia did the same thing."

The breath caught in my throat. I glanced at Stephanie.

"I'll see you at dinner," Mom said. "Colin and I want to take you guys to Ye Olde Train Depot for dinner. Our treat."

"All right," I said and looked down at the sapphire ring on my finger.

With that, Colin turned her chair and wheeled her down the street.

"I'm glad you're here, Stephanie," I said and took her hand.

She squeezed. "I can hardly wait."

"For what?"

"We're going to have so many adventures," she said. "Now that I'll be part of the historical society and giving tours. We'll be like the Pershing sisters all over again. I'm Wilma and you're Sylvia."

"Oh," I said, laughing. "How come you get to be the nice one?"

"Well, you get to be the skinny one," she said and smiled.

"I guess I should get back to work."

"What about that newspaper article? You know, the one that columnist guy wrote?" she asked.

"Oh, believe me, if you say 'that newspaper article,' I know which one you're referring to. Collette got him to write a retraction.

It's going to run tomorrow. He's going to say that maybe his own biased opinion made him draw a few not so generous conclusions about me and New Kassel. Whatever his bias is. I haven't a clue. I don't really care. As long as he prints it."

"People can really cause a ruckus," Stephanie said.

"I know." We turned to go into the Gaheimher House, but before I had a chance to go back to work, my mother-in-law came walking down the street. Priscilla O'Shea had her hair perfectly coiffed, and there was not one wrinkle anywhere in her clothes. How did she do that? Did she somehow manage to stay straight while she was sitting down?

"I'll be inside," Stephanie said. Just like that, she left me on the steps alone.

"Torie," Mrs. O'Shea said.

I immediately bristled. I knew she was going to attack me over something. But I had already vowed not to let her get to me. In fact, I was going to apologize to her. "Priscilla," I said.

"I . . . I want you to know . . ."

Lord, was she trying to apologize to me instead?

"You look terrible."

"Thank you," I said. Some things never change, I suppose.

"What do you think you're teaching your children?"

"Priscilla," I said and held up my hands. "Stop."

"What?" she said.

"I want to call a truce," I said.

"A truce?"

"I know we haven't always . . ." Liked each other. "Seen eye to eye."

She said nothing. She just crossed her arms.

"But really, this constant bickering and belittling isn't helping anything. In fact, that's a lesson I'd just as soon not teach my children," I said. "I know you want what's best for your son. So do I."

She rolled her eyes and made a huffing noise.

"See, the thing is, Rudy's his own man. If he were truly unhappy, he'd do something about it," I said. She started to protest, but I spoke over her. "And if he doesn't do anything about it, then it's nobody's fault but his own. You can't blame me for Rudy being unhappy. If Rudy is somewhere he doesn't want to be, living a lie or living in a manner he doesn't like . . . well, he's a big boy. He can fix it. And if he can't fix it, then that's his shortcoming."

That stopped her.

"You can't run people's lives forever," I said. "In fact, you'd enjoy your own life so much more if you'd stop trying to be the mayor of everybody else's life. Now, I am really, truly sorry, Priscilla, if I have ever done anything to offend you. I apologize for being born in a hick county. This whole week, I have been the biggest jerk to you. I was asinine, I know. But you waltzed in here and started throwing insults and, well, I got defensive."

She said nothing. She only stared at me as if I'd grown two heads. Maybe it was just that I'd grown a new head. One she'd never seen before.

"I won't do this anymore," I said and crossed my arms. "There is nothing you can say that will get me to behave this badly again."

She was speechless.

I was uncomfortable.

"Do you forgive me?" I asked.

"Y-yes," she said. "I forgive you."

"Good, because I forgive you, too." It was pretty clear by the expression on her face that she wasn't entirely certain that she had done anything to be forgiven for.

"If you'll excuse me," I said. "There's something I have to do."

"Of course," she said.

"Oh, one more thing. Do you think you could make those stuffed mushroom thingies for dinner tonight? Nobody makes them like you," I said.

Her shoulders relaxed. The lines between her eyes disappeared. And a smile—however fragile it may have been—spread across her face. "Sure," she said.

I stared down at Sylvia's grave. It was too early for the tombstone to be finished, so the only thing marking her grave was a little metal signpost and some fresh dirt. I would have known it was hers no matter what, though. It was right next to her sister's grave. I held a bouquet of daisies in one hand and her emerald green scarf in the other.

"I'm not sure if I'll be able to forgive you for this, Sylvia," I said to the pile of dirt. "For all of it." And I meant it. My mother was right. Money did change those around you, but it had changed me just a little bit, too. I had become defensive and a little more aloof with the other people in town since inheriting Sylvia's money and property. I'd become more guarded. What did they want from me? There it was, that question in the back of my mind. Did they hate me for being rich? Obviously, the answer had been yes for some. And Sylvia had given me all of that.

She had also given me what—aside from my family—I loved the most. The Gaheimer House. The historical society. And in a way, she'd given me New Kassel, too. I'm not sure I would have ever looked at this town as its own entity, with its own personality. Sylvia had showed me that. Every town has it. It's a matter of whether you can see past the concrete and the wood and the electrical lines and feel it. Can you hear it speaking to you? Sylvia had shown me that when I was a young girl, and I would be forever grateful.

"But I'll try to forgive you. I promise."

Then there was Millie O'Shaughnessy, the small German-Irish girl who happened to have drawn a less than ideal lot in life. I could only imagine her mother's anguish, knowing that she had consumption and knowing that there was nobody to raise her daughter— and then the one person she trusted agreed to take her. Theodora O'Shaughnessy had died at peace, thinking her daughter would be taken care of.

But then, as it often does, life threw a curveball. Things didn't work out quite like they were supposed to. I had no idea what happened to Millie between the ages of six and seventeen, when she married Mr. Trotter. I had no idea what she ate, where she slept, how she managed to stay warm. Knowing what I know about orphans in America during the Depression, it probably wasn't anything I would want to experience. And it was all because of Sylvia.

Why had Sylvia broken her promise? I like to think that there had been a breakdown of communication, that somehow Sylvia had agreed to take the girl, and then wires got crossed and the girl was gone, and Sylvia was free of guilt. But I knew in my heart that very likely wasn't the case. And it killed me.

I think you have forgotten your promise.

I would never forget it. Millie's face was burned on my mind forever, and so were those haunting and tragic words.

Tears spilled down my face, and I wiped them away with Sylvia's scarf.

A group of loud teenagers went running by, laughing and horsing around. One of those noisy teenagers was my daughter Rachel. She saw me, said a few words to her friends, and jumped over the fence of the cemetery. Of course she couldn't use the gate. She was a teenager. She ran up to me and looked down at Sylvia's grave.

"Are you all right?" she asked.

"No," I said. "I just don't know how she could have done it. And how she could have lived with it."

"Are you talking about Helen's grandma?" she asked. I nodded. I had told her all about it the night before, along with the story of Deputy Duran. "Seems kinda silly. Duran, I mean."

"People have killed for a lot less, Rachel. A lot less. It's not that silly."

I sniffed and wondered how many more tears I would shed because of Sylvia. Rachel placed her head on my shoulder and rubbed my back. You spend years comforting your children, holding them while they cry, picking them up when they fall. It's unsettling when they get old enough to return the favor. But thank God they're *there* to return the favor.

"I think it's like that *White Ship* and Henry," Rachel said.

"What do you mean?"

"You know, Henry the First. Remember that story you told me? How his only legitimate son was killed on the *White Ship*, because Henry was king, and if Henry had never killed his brother to become king, his son William would have probably lived."

"You are totally confusing me. Besides, they don't know for sure that Henry killed his brother."

"But if he did, and he most likely did, then it was that action that led directly to William going down on the *White Ship*."

"Right. I already said that. What has that got to do with Sylvia?"

She shrugged. "Sylvia's actions almost cost you your life. She thought she was giving you everything, and she nearly took it all away," she said. "And Helen. If Sylvia had adopted her grandmother, none of this would have happened. She would have had a daughter to leave everything to. It wouldn't have gone to you."

A tear dropped from my face and landed on the fresh dirt. I threw the daisies onto Sylvia's grave and then hugged my daughter. "You're pretty smart," I said. "Wonder where you got that?"

"Grandma O said it came from her."

"Ahh," I said.

•

I walked into Fräulein Krista's Speisehaus, waved to Krista, and reveled in the crowd that was gathered. I walked over to the big stuffed bear at the end of the bar. The town mascot, our big stuffed grizzly bear named Sylvia. Ferocious, stubborn, but a born protector of those she loved. I tied the emerald green scarf around its neck, turned, and walked out into the streets that I adored so much.

Everything would be all right. I was suddenly overcome with a sense of well-being. But there was one more thing I needed to do before I could sleep at night.

Fifteen minutes later I found Helen working at the berry booth. She waved when she saw me, but not with a great amount of enthusiasm. I motioned for her, and she stepped outside the booth and over to me. "Whatcha need?"

"I . . . I need your forgiveness," I said.

She stared at me for a second, I suppose trying to see if I was serious or not. Then she crossed her arms. She was going to make me work for this, and I can't say that I didn't deserve it.

"I am so sorry for everything, Helen. In my own defense I will say that I was so hurt by what happened at the meeting that I don't think I was myself for a few days. I think if I hadn't seen you right away, if you'd waited a few days before you came around, I would have never said those things that I said. I was hurt. Plain and simple. I don't think I've ever been that hurt," I said. "But still, that's no excuse."

Helen nodded.

"And I'm also sorry for suspecting you. After I talked to you and learned . . . well, learned everything about your family and the connection with Sylvia, I connected that with what happened at the meeting, and I suspected you of being the one trying to run me out of town. I am so sorry, Helen, not to mention a little ashamed of myself. My only excuse is that I think I've been on the verge of an emotional breakdown since Sylvia died. This has been so stressful. Not to mention the whole mother-in-law thing."

She said nothing.

"I promise I will never suspect you of trying to kill me again. Unless you *are* trying to kill me, at which time I'd probably deserve it."

She smiled then and unfolded her arms. "You big nincompoop," she said and hugged me. "I can't believe you would really think I would try to run you out of town. I mean, the last time the mayor tried to get rid of you, I stuck up for you!"

"Oh, thanks," I said.

She laughed and took a deep breath. "Torie, I . . . I really was not the most supportive at the meeting," she said. "I was . . . I, just thought, 'Wow, they're really going to overthrow the dynasty,' and I would just slip in and be president without anybody noticing."

"Helen—"

"No, really. It was wrong of me, and so you're not entirely to blame here. You really were reading weird vibes from me, because I really was thinking them. So I guess if you can forgive me for riding on the shirttails of a coup, I can forgive you for assuming I wanted you to move to Alaska."

"Okay, we're even," I said. "Now I just have one more thing."

"What's that?"

"Is there anything you need? Anything you want?"

"You mean from Sylvia's things?"

I nodded.

"No, Torie. My husband has spent the better part of twenty-five years telling me I'm stubborn, and he doesn't lie. My family never took anything from Sylvia when she was alive. I'm not going to start now."

"All right," I said. "You better get back to work."

"Yeah," she said.

"Oh, one more thing, Helen."

"What's that?"

"Do you think my tenants would like to have their houses?"

Helen stared at me for a moment, and then a very warm and generous smile spread across her face. She ran back over and hugged me again. This time she squeezed me so hard my ears popped. "Don't let anybody ever tell you that you're Sylvia Pershing," she said. "Not ever."

She went back to work, and I turned to leave. I walked down the street toward the crowd that had gathered at the pie-eating booth, with a bounce in my step and a light heart. Even without those houses, I still had more money than I ever dreamed I would have. The Gaheimer House was mine. I could give tours forever. As I walked along, I really felt as though there was nothing from here on out that could deter me from having a perfectly charmed life in my beautiful peaceful small town. The sun would shine forever. Maybe I'd take up tai chi or yoga.

I made my way through the crowd to see that the pie-eating contest had started. It was the usual suspects: Rudy, Colin, and Chuck, all with their faces down in the pies. It looked like they had some stiff competition with some of the tourists. Then again, one chap was actually eating his pie with a fork and napkin tucked in his shirt. Boy, was he in for a rude awakening.

When the contest was over, Oscar Murdoch raised the hand of the winner.

My husband. He let out a war whoop, with both fists raised above his head and strawberry goo all down the front of his shirt. Yes, things were back to normal in New Kassel. Different, but normal.

Rudy took the microphone from Oscar. "I'd like to thank everybody who made these pies," he said. He pointed at me and winked. "I love you, Torie."

"I want a rematch!" Chuck yelled.

"Oh, hey," Colin said and grabbed the microphone. "I'd just like to say . . . I'm running for mayor!"

Oh. Lord. Help. Me.

FIC MacPherson, Rett.
Macphers
Thicker than water.

22.95

DATE				
		MAR 0 5		

BAKER & TAYLOR